About the Author

CLINT WATTS is a Robert A. Fox Fellow in the Foreign Policy Research Institute's Program on the Middle East as well as a senior fellow at the Center for Cyber and Homeland Security at the George Washington University.

The
Elevator
Ghost

GLEN HUSER

Illustrations by Stacy Innerst

GROUNDWOOD BOOKS
HOUSE OF ANANSI PRESS
TORONTO / BERKELEY

Thank you to my editor, Shelley Tanaka.
If anyone knows how to sort out the bones of a story, she does.

Text copyright © 2014 by Glen Huser
Published in Canada and the USA in 2014 by Groundwood Books

Groundwood Books/House of Anansi Press
110 Spadina Avenue, Suite 801
Toronto, Ontario M5V 2K4
or c/o Publishers Group West
1700 Fourth Street, Berkeley, CA 94710

We acknowledge for their financial support of our publishing program the
Canada Council for the Arts, the Government of Canada through the Canada
Book Fund (CBF) and the Ontario Arts Council.

Canada Council   Conseil des Arts
for the Arts   du Canada

ONTARIO ARTS COUNCIL
CONSEIL DES ARTS DE L'ONTARIO

Library and Archives Canada Cataloguing in Publication
Huser, Glen, author
The elevator ghost / by Glen Huser.

Issued in print and electronic formats.
ISBN 978-1-55498-425-1 (bound).—ISBN 978-1-55498-426-8 (pbk.).—
ISBN 978-1-55498-427-5 (html)

I. Title.

PS8565.U823E44 2014   jC813'.54   C2014-900900-3

C2014-900901-1

Cover illustration by Stacy Innerst
Design by Michael Solomon

Printed and bound in Canada

For
Story
Xander
Kasey
Maggie
Isla
Aislyn
Beau
Laila

ONE

Halloween Night

BLATCHFORD WAS SCARY any night of the year, not just on Halloween. It was a very old part of town with crooked streets and bad lighting. Cats yowled and scrapped in the alleys. Teenagers with tattoos were known to hang out under the bridges by the park.

In the middle of it all, a huge apartment building loomed like a castle, darkened with age. The Blatchford Arms poked up above all the buildings around. When there was a full moon, it looked as though the building's two towers were nibbling at it.

Some said the place was haunted.

October 31st, while there were very few children wandering around the streets in Blatchford, things were different inside the apartment building. Children (and a few dogs) raced along the hallways. The costumed kids rang doorbells and shouted, "Halloween apples!" They clattered up and down the staircases. Some rode the elevator, which squealed and groaned like a creature in pain.

"Quit playing with that elevator," Herman Spiegelman, the caretaker, growled at the Lubinitsky girls. There were always move-outs on the last day of the month. Herman had a big job ahead of him, getting Apartment 713 cleaned and ready for a new tenant.

"Don't you be drawing nothing on these walls." He shook a mop handle at the smallest Lubinitsky, who did in fact have a black crayon clutched in her free hand. "One mark and a monster with sharp teeth'll come and gobble you up while you're sleeping."

Three floors down, the Bellini sisters tried to coax their little brother, Angelo, away from a basket of cookies old Mrs. Floss had left on a stand outside her door.

"No! Mine!" he shrieked. He began to jump up and down, trying to grab more cookies even though his hands were already full.

Amanita Bellini yanked at his Dracula cape while Corrina rescued the basket and held it out of reach.

"The sign says 'Help yourself to a cookie!'" She tried to make herself heard over his howls. "That means one. One cookie."

By this time Mrs. Floss had opened her door. She waved her cane at Angelo. She was very old and had a creaky voice, but the girls managed to hear her say, "That boy should be locked up in a cage in the basement."

Meanwhile, the Hooper kids had worked their way from the top of the building down to the second floor. Benjamin, dressed as a spaceship, was having some trouble with the narrow halls. His sisters, one on each side, helped to steer him. They had just spent half an hour fixing a display he had bumped into. Six plastic skeletons and a full-size Frankenstein outside the Murplestein apartment had toppled and scattered along the hallway.

"Why can't you dress like something normal," Lucy Hooper grumbled. "Like Batman or Raggedy Andy."

"Or a peanut," Emma Hooper added.

Hubert and Hetty Croop, costumed as salt and pepper shakers, had only managed to get down to the end of their own hall when everything went dark. They would have grabbed onto each other for support, but that was not especially easy for salt and pepper shakers to do. Hubert tripped over Hetty's feet, fell and began to roll this way and that. Hetty tried to get down on her knees to help, but the stiff cardboard of her costume made that difficult.

Some eerie shrieks sent them scrambling back along the hall.

By the time the lights came on, they were both huddled against their apartment door, whimpering.

The door opened.

Mrs. Croop gasped. "Come here, Sylvester," she called to her husband. "Our children have been attacked!"

The Fergus twins, Dwayne and Dwight, were faster than any other children in the building. They had already visited all the floors of the Blatchford Arms. Their pillowcases were half-filled with treats when they burst out the front doors.

Nothing — rats in the alleys, teens pierced like pincushions, loose dogs or whiskered bin-divers — was going to stop them from filling their stash-bags with candy.

In Blatchford, there weren't a lot of houses with their porch lights on to welcome roving ghouls and goblins, but the twins knew exactly where to find them.

After what seemed like hours combing the streets, Dwight lifted up his rubber Scream mask to get a breath of air.

"What time is it?"

"Who cares?" Dwayne poked his brother with the long spiky fingernails on his Freddy Krueger glove.

Dwight scooped up a half-eaten apple someone had dropped on the sidewalk and chucked it at Dwayne. It fell into his bag of treats.

"Hey!" Dwayne yanked Dwight's mask until it stretched out to nearly twice its size. Then he let it snap back.

If the boys hadn't been so busy arguing, they might have noticed a car creeping along the street beside them.

Inside the car, Carolina Giddle sighed and shook her head so that the crystal globes dangling from her ears spun around.

The truth was, she was lost. As she tried to look at a street map and steer, she wasn't moving much faster than the boys. The streets in Blatchford always confounded visitors, leading them to dead ends along the park or onto bridges that spanned the very place a person wanted to be.

When Carolina Giddle had last been in Blatchford, many years ago, she hadn't owned a car. She had taken a rickety old bus to visit her great-aunt Beulah in the Blatchford seniors' home.

Since then, Aunt Beulah, at 102, had passed on. Shortly before she died, she wrote her niece a letter. Carolina Giddle kept it tucked in her back pocket like a good-luck charm. She knew it by heart.

Dear Niece Carolina,

Hope you are well and, as they say, the hens are all laying and the creek ain't run dry.

I wanted to let you know that I was able to visit the Arms where I used to live before I was married. I'd been having a strong notion to go there so Gertie wheeled me over in my chair.

You remember me telling you about my friend Grace who died from the consumption? When Gertie went to get herself a coffee, Grace came and sat with me in the sunroom. I told her about how you were on the prowl to find a place these days. Grace was looking good, I thought, for someone who's been dead for 83 years. Anyway, she said, "You tell your niece to come on here soon as there's a vacancy. The rent's cheap." She said she can always use a friend with a good sense of the spirit world, and there's a passel of families that'd shuck out good money for someone to mind the children when there's a need. So I'm passing on her message.

I'd ask you to come and live with me at the home, but the rooms are about the size of a tea bag. At the Arms, though, you'll be close by for visits.

With love,

Aunt Beulah

That had been the last letter from Aunt Beulah. And now there would be someone else living in her tiny room at the seniors' home.

Carolina Giddle came to a full stop. She sighed again and dabbed at a tear. Then she patted something about the size of a shoebox on the seat beside her. It was covered with a red bandana.

"Are you awake, Chiquita?" Carolina Giddle whispered. "Saints preserve us, will you look at that. I've been holding the map upside down. Why, we just need to turn left at this next corner."

The parking lot outside the Blatchford Arms was calm and quiet. Moonlight washed over the cars, trucks and motorcycles. It added some sly glitter to the eyes of a black cat exploring garbage that had spilled from the dumpsters at the edge of the lot.

Dwight and Dwayne were back now. Dwight pulled off his Scream mask and poured a boxful of Smarties into his mouth. Dwayne poked a toothbrush a dentist's family had been handing out into his brother's ear, nearly making him choke.

"Cut it out, scumbag!" Dwight coughed up a couple of Smarties to spit at his twin.

They had been told by their parents to be back at eight-thirty at the latest. Being two and a half hours late already, they weren't especially anxious to get home.

"Maybe Ma and Pa have gone over to the Murplesteins." Dwayne plunged his hand into his pillowcase, searching for chocolate bars.

"Don't count on it. The old man's going to be waiting there with his belt off." Dwight gave his brother a knowing look. They had both taken the precaution of padding their backsides with all the underwear they owned.

Their dad had never actually used his belt on them, but he'd threatened often.

It didn't hurt to be prepared. Just in case.

"Long as he don't snatch our treats," Dwayne muttered.

The boys were about ready to move on when their attention was caught by something large and lumpy easing its way past them. It was quite unlike anything they had ever seen before.

It looked like a huge pile of furniture that was moving mysteriously by itself. Somewhere, from its core, was the sound of an engine sputtering. As it wheezed past, it became evident that beneath the heap of chair legs, a bureau without any drawers, a rolled-up mattress, a

coffee table, some plant-holders and cardboard boxes of different sizes — all tied together with bits of colored cloth and rope — there was in fact a car. A Volkswagen bug.

But not just an ordinary VW.

It was a bug whose surface — at least any bits showing beneath the mountain of furniture and boxes — was entirely covered with small objects. It looked to the boys like there were tiny figurines and Tinkertoys, fridge magnets, bits of jewelry, Christmas decorations and spoons with fancy handles.

Every square inch was covered with knickknacks.

The car was moving so slowly that the boys had no trouble following it to the Blatchford Arms' front entrance, where it stopped in the No Parking zone.

Without saying a word, they donned their masks. Dwayne was once again a small Freddy Krueger. Dwight pulled the black hood of his jacket up tight to show off his Scream mask.

After all, it was still Halloween. Anyone creeping around a parking lot in a scabbed-up bug groaning under a heap of furniture should have a proper welcome.

Dwayne gave Dwight a friendly poke with his elbow, and both boys snickered.

The VW's door creaked open, and someone got out. Hiding behind Mr. Spiegelman's truck, the twins found it hard to see clearly with their masks in place. They could only make out the person's back.

Was it a man or a woman?

They heard the car door close. The person turned around.

It was a woman. Not exactly an old woman, but not a young one, either. A mess of hair escaped from beneath a straw hat, making her look a bit like a scarecrow the twins had seen on a class trip to a farm. A scarecrow with bright red lipstick and a red bandana around her neck. Peeking out at the bottom of her overalls were feet clad in tennis shoes with sequins glittering across their toes. It looked like she had crystal marbles hanging from her ears.

The boys had been planning to jump out from behind the truck making terrible yelling noises. But it took them a minute to drink in the strangeness of the woman by the Volkswagen.

In that minute, she turned and looked right where they were hiding. Her mouth widened in a huge smile.

"When you're ready to come out, I would be mighty obliged if you'd hold the door open while I move in my possessions." The woman had a voice with a sound to it that Dwight and Dwayne had only ever heard on TV. A voice from somewhere in the South, where there were maybe cotton fields and big trees dripping with Spanish moss.

Dwayne rose up from behind the truck's fender.

How did this woman know they were hiding?

Dwight let out a kind of pitiful yelp. He sounded like his dog Barkus getting his tail stepped on. Not like a monster about to attack.

"Oh, my!" The woman clasped a hand to the bib of her overalls and chuckled. She wore red fingernail polish that matched her lipstick. "Y'all are a most frightful sight."

Dwight pulled off his mask and dropped it on top of the treats in his pillowcase.

"You moving in?"

"I surely am." The scarecrow woman reached in and pulled something from the passenger seat. It was a mesh cage partly covered by a bandana like the one she was wearing.

She handed it to Dwight.

24

"Would you mind? This is Chiquita. If you're steady and very gentle, I think we can get her inside without waking her."

"Chiquita?" Dwayne had abandoned his mask now, too.

"My pet tarantula," the woman said.

When Dwight and Dwayne finally got to their apartment on the fifth floor, Mr. Fergus was waiting with his belt off.

Dwight gulped. Dwayne dropped his pillowcase of goodies behind the umbrella stand.

"Do you have anything to say before I whup the living daylights out of you?" Mr. Fergus gave his belt a couple of light practice smacks against the palm of his hand.

"Don't take too long, dear," Mrs. Fergus called from the kitchen. "If we go right away, we can still catch the tail end of the Murplesteins' party."

"What have you got to say for yourselves?" Mr. Fergus growled.

"Well, sir…" Dwayne took a deep breath. "We would have been home almost on time but there was this poor little old lady getting ready to move in just when we got to the downstairs door."

"She asked us would we give her some help." Dwight suddenly found his voice. "I think we must've made about a hundred trips up to her apartment."

"You know the one." Dwight mopped a hand over his brow, hoping that there was at least a little bit of sweat there. "Where Billy Crimpey used to live."

The truth was that the twins had only made one trip up to Apartment 713, carrying the tarantula cage and something weird and glassy with lumps of color burping around in it. Carolina Giddle called it a lava lamp. It was all they could manage and still hang onto their pillowcases of Halloween loot.

That's when the scarecrow lady met Mr. Spiegelman.

"The suite's not ready until November 1st," the caretaker grumbled, standing in the middle of a small pile of what looked like pink stone chips, but Dwight recognized as a petrified form of Billy Crimpey's favorite bubblegum.

"Well…" The scarecrow lady checked her watch and smiled at Mr. Spiegelman. "It'll be November 1st in about thirty-eight minutes. The apartment's looking pretty spic and span to me, but I could give you a hand if there's any last-minute scrubbing to do."

Both Dwight and Dwayne were ready to see how the standoff between the building's super and the scarecrow lady would go, but Mr. Spiegelman waved his chisel at them and shooed them away.

"Thank you kindly, boys," the lady said. "You give your papa and mama one of my cards if you don't mind." She reached into a huge handbag she was carrying and pulled out a business card.

Now Dwight fished around for the card and found it stuck to a piece of toffee.

"Here. She said to give you this." He pinched off the toffee and gazed up at his father with a practiced look of innocence.

"Are you finished, dear?" Mrs. Fergus emerged from the kitchen, wiping her hands on her apron. "Gladys Murplestein just phoned and said there's no way they can serve my vampire cake unless we're there to cut it. First cut, right through the count's heart."

"The boys were helping an old lady move." Mr. Fergus didn't sound very convinced, but he threaded his belt back through the loops on his pants. "Here, she gave you this."

"Hmm…" Mrs. Fergus held up the card to

the hall light. "*Carolina Giddle. Experienced babysitter, mah-jong instructor and vegetarian caterer. Will do light housekeeping and séances upon request.* Fancy that."

"Sounds like a fruitcake to me," said Mr. Fergus.

"We do need a babysitter next month." Mrs. Fergus looked at her boys, sighed and shook her head. "Millicent's wedding, remember? And no one in the building will babysit here anymore."

"I ain't no baby," Dwayne complained.

"No backlip." Mr. Fergus made a threatening movement toward his belt buckle. "You two get to bed and you better not get out of bed if you know what's good for you."

With her gaze focused on the hall mirror, Mrs. Fergus ran a comb through her hair.

"I'm going to be sneakin' back every ten minutes from the Murplesteins. If I catch you..." Mr. Fergus pointed a finger in the direction of the boys' bedroom. "And Mrs. Griddle or whatever *is* goin' to babysit you while me and your ma are at Auntie Millicent's wedding. BABY-sit, you hear?"

———————

An hour past midnight, all of the excitement over Halloween had faded away. There was just the smallest taste of it left, like the sweetness from a caramel. Children had fallen asleep, even those complaining of stomachaches.

Galina Lubinitsky still clutched her crayon, bits of it rubbing off onto her pillow. Mrs. Croop, hearing Hubert's small snores, switched off his bedroom light. He could never go to sleep unless it was on. Papa Bellini sighed and shook his head as he pulled a blanket up tight to Angelo's chin. Asleep, he did look like an angel. Benjamin Hooper's model spaceships, hanging from his bedroom ceiling, twirled in a shaft of moonglow.

In Apartment 713, Carolina Giddle brewed a pot of tea.

"It will be ready in two shakes," she announced to Herman Spiegelman as he unloaded a trolley with the last of her things. "Huckleberry peppermint, and I add just a splash of Southern Comfort. Especially good with one of my granghoula bars, which I think I have packed right there in that top box if you'll hand it to me."

"It's been a long day." Herman Spiegelman mopped his brow. He settled into a caneback chair by the drop-leaf table Carolina Giddle was opening up. "They should pass a law against Halloween."

"I would miss it like a good back tooth," Carolina Giddle said. She added an extra splash from a bottle into the super's tea. "There." She handed it to him.

The caretaker took a deep, satisfying sip. "You come from a long ways?"

"Yes, I reckon it's the longest trip Trinket and I've ever made, and I've had her for twenty-two years."

"Trinket?"

"My car."

"Trinket." Herman Spiegelman tasted the word along with a bite of granghoula bar. "Never seen a vehicle quite so…" He stopped and searched for a word. "Decorated. And what brings you here?"

"I have friends…" Carolina Giddle paused and smiled as she slowly stirred some honey into her tea.

There was a sudden clanking from the radiator. And then what sounded like a clearing of a throat.

Cough. Cough.

"Oh, be quiet, you consarn whatever." The caretaker settled his teacup carefully on the table, pulled a wrench from his overall pocket and delivered a blow that made the old radiator vibrate and ring.

The clanking and the coughing stopped.

Carolina Giddle's eyebrows made little peaks, and she bit her lip. After Herman Spiegelman had finished his tea, collected his trolley and said goodnight, she went over and stood by the radiator. She gave it a gentle pat.

There was a cough again. So soft you could barely hear it. And the radiator gurgled contentedly for a minute or two.

"Hello, Grace," Carolina Giddle whispered. "Don't worry. It's just me."

TWO

The Bone Game

THE TWELFTH OF November was a Saturday. It was a warm fall day. There was just enough breeze to send the last poplar leaves skittering across the hills and hollows of the park.

Dwight and Dwayne spent all day in the park. There was plenty to do. They played Ante I Over the tea pavilion roof until their softball hit a gardener on the head and he chased them away. They dropped water bombs on joggers from a low-hanging branch on a chestnut tree.

But the most fun was hiding in a culvert

close to where Hubert and Hetty Croop were collecting leaves for a school project.

Dwight and Dwayne knew how easy it was to frighten the living daylights out of the Croop kids. Their best prank had been scaring them with a fake rat. That still made them whoop with laughter. Dwight had taken Barkus's favorite squeak-toy and tucked it inside an old moth-eaten fur muff he found in a garbage bin. While Dwight hid around a corner, Dwayne waited for Hubert and Hetty to get off the elevator on their way home from school.

"You guys seen that rat that's been running loose on your floor?" Dwayne asked them.

"Rat!" Hubert clutched Hetty's coat sleeve.

Then Dwight came out and ran at them, hollering and waving the squeaking piece of fur. "Help! It's got me! It's chewing off my arm!"

Hubert and Hetty ran away howling with

fear, stumbling through the Exit door and down the fire escape.

To find Croop kids in the park by themselves was almost as good as finding dropped money.

Hetty was just reaching into the edge of the culvert to grab a red maple leaf when the boys let out roars that would have frightened a grizzly bear.

Hetty screamed and Hubert yelped. Their leaves went flying as they raced for the park gate. Dwight and Dwayne burst out of the culvert and ran from tree to tree, hiding behind the trunks and roaring.

Once the Croops were out of sight, the twins lay on the leaf-spattered grass and held their sides, laughing.

They were still chuckling when they got home. With all the fun they'd been having, they'd forgotten that they were being left in the care of Carolina Giddle for the evening.

"What the… " Dwight choked on the laugh that had gurgled up again as he opened the apartment door.

"Huh." Dwayne shook his head.

Carolina Giddle perched on a stool in the kitchen. Her flyaway scarecrow hair was caught up with a clip that looked like a coiled silver snake. She wore a shirt that seemed to be covered with little black lizards with sequin eyes.

"How lovely to see you two again," Carolina Giddle said in that special way she had of talking. As if she were dragging her words through honey. "Dee-wight and Dee-wayne, isn't it?"

Dwayne glared. "We don't need no babysitter."

Mr. Fergus rubbed his thumb against his belt loop and gave them his don't-mess-with-me look.

"You be good for Ms. Giddle." Mrs. Fergus blew kisses at the boys as they headed out.

With their parents gone, the Fergus twins gave one another knowing looks. It was a silent signal to get busy with all of the tricks they'd played on babysitters over the years.

When Carolina Giddle dished tomato soup for their supper, Dwight quickly splashed a big dollop of Louisiana hot sauce into her bowl when her back was turned. Enough to send her screaming for water.

Carolina Giddle took a spoonful, then smiled and said, "I think I'll just add a bit of hot sauce to mine." She removed the cap, up-ended the bottle and said, "Mm...mm," as it drizzled into her soup. "Where I come from, they say this will put curl into your hair! You boys care for some?"

As Carolina did up the dishes, the boys lured Barkus, their pet sheepdog, into a bath-tub laced with the contents of a full bottle of bubble bath. Soon there were bubbles oozing down the hall from the bathroom.

But Carolina Giddle simply said, "Oh, my. I love to see boys and dogs clean as a Sunday-go-to-meeting shirt."

She plugged in a fan and blew all of the bubbles back into the bathroom, where she opened a window. Clouds of soap bubbles drifted out into the night, and the boys took turns watching the surprised looks of pass-ersby on the street below.

Meanwhile Carolina Giddle dried Barkus gently with a huge towel, and he gave her several appreciative licks on her hand.

The twins were pretty tired by this time, so their attempt to stage a fight, complete with ketchup for fake blood, wasn't really their best effort. Still, there was a good chance that Carolina Giddle might faint at the sight of so much blood. Or she might get hysterical and call an ambulance.

Instead, she dipped her finger into the blood, tasted it and said, "I think this could use some hot sauce, too."

"I'm gonna watch a movie on TV," Dwayne declared when she told them it was time to get ready for bed. He and Dwight flung themselves onto the couch in the living room and began fighting — for real this time — over the remote control.

And that's when all the lights went off, and the TV died in the living room.

"Hey!" the twins shouted.

In the next minute Carolina Giddle stood silhouetted in the light from the kitchen door.

"Jumpin' junebugs!" she said. "Looks like a couple of fuses have blown. But never mind, I'll tell you a story instead."

"That's for babies," Dwight grumbled.

"Well, you don't need to listen, but I'm in the mood for telling. I think this dim light is what's putting it in my mind. I'll just get out my candles."

She eased herself onto the other end of the couch.

"It's a ghost story," she added, lighting several tea candles and arranging them in a circle on an end table. She reached into her bag and drew out the cage with the tarantula in it. Chiquita looked up at the twins and seemed to wave one of her hairy arms in greeting.

"Chiquita hates to miss a good ghost story," Carolina Giddle noted. "And, oh, yes. I nearly forgot. I've brought along a snack — some bone rattlers. They're from a favorite recipe of my grandmother's. She always had some on hand when I visited her for the holidays."

"Bone rattlers?" The twins sometimes said the same thing at the same time, and this was one of those times.

Carolina Giddle fetched a plastic container

out of her handbag, snapping the lid free. She pulled out some white items that looked like a skeleton's finger bones. They glistened in the candlelight. A delicious smell of peppermint filled the air.

The boys watched as Carolina Giddle crunched into one of the treats and sighed between chews.

"Mmm-mmm, so deelish," she said, picking a bit of peppermint out of her front teeth.

Dwight reached over and got a bone rattler for himself. He slipped a sliver of it into Chiquita's cage.

"She's not a vegetarian," Carolina Giddle said. "But she does love the smell of peppermint."

Dwayne's fingers curled around a bone rattler, too, as he dropped the remote and leaned back against his brother.

The tea lights flickered in the dark room. Everything was quiet as a grave, except for

the sound of the boys crunching their treats,
and Carolina Giddle began.

*Some ghost stories are old as a Chattahoochee
levee and others can spring up — why, even yes-
terday. I heard this one a couple of years ago. It
was told to me by an old woman who lived on a
little island in the swamp country on the edge of
town, just back of the Chattahoochee River.*

*Seems there were two boys. Jimmy Joe and
Oren lived no more than a hop, skip and a holler
from the old woman. Those boys — I think they
were about nine years old — were up to constant
devilment. Especially whenever there was a full
moon.*

*The boys had been watching TV news and
had heard about a running shoe washing up on
a beach someplace hundreds of miles away. A
single running shoe with bones from a human
foot in it, and no way of telling where they might
have come from.*

43

Wouldn't it be a good joke, the boys thought, to get hold of an old running shoe and put some bones in it and leave it on the levee right where someone would be bound to find it.

Where would they get the bones, they wondered. Maybe coyote bones or buzzard bones from the swamp?

But Jimmy Joe had a better idea. His daddy was a caretaker at the medical school downtown on the green. It was easy enough for him to go with his father one of the nights he was at work.

There were a couple of skeletons out in the laboratories, but Jimmy Joe was lucky enough to find one stored away in a closet — yes, sometimes there is a skeleton in a closet — and he guessed this was one nobody would be looking at for some time.

So he snipped the wires holding that foot to the leg bone and made off with it.

Sure enough, a fisherman found the running shoe and took it to the police station. The TV and newspapers got all excited. They became even more excited when a forensic expert informed them the bones were about a hundred years old.

Although they lived on different streets running down to the levee, Oren and Jimmy Joe liked to meet up in the wee small hours of the morning when the world was sleeping and they should have been, too. It was as easy as falling off a log for them to slip out of their upstairs bedroom windows and shinny down a drainpipe or a tree. Sometimes they ran from street to street ringing doorbells. Sometimes they hid behind fences making horrible noises like cats fighting, until people woke up and threw things at them. Sometimes they rambled through the park in the middle of town, chucking stones at the trash barrels or tying the playground swings in knots.

A couple of nights after they put the skeleton's foot in a running shoe, the boys arranged to meet at the edge of the park across from the medical school. Jimmy Joe's daddy had fin-

ished his janitor work hours earlier, and all of the lights were off.

Or so it seemed.

Oren was sprawled against a trunk of one of those big old park trees, laughing as he showed Jimmy Joe a clipping from the morning newspaper featuring the shoe and the ankle joint sticking out of it.

But Jimmy Joe wasn't laughing. He clutched Oren's arm and pointed to the medical school. The boys could see a dim light in one of the upper-floor windows. Then the light was in the next window along the hallway. And then the next one, moving from room to room.

"What in tarnation…" Oren's voice croaked like an old frog in the swamp.

The light disappeared. Then it reappeared at a window on the lower floor, and another window, moving toward the front door.

Just then a cloud covered the moon and everything was suddenly as dark as the inside of a gunny sack. The boys held their breath. They wanted to run, but something kept them there. They were frozen with fear. But they also wanted to see what the moonlight would reveal once that cloud drifted by.

What they saw was the light appearing at the top of the stairs outside the front door of the medical school. It was a candle. And it was held in a bony hand by a skeleton.

When the skeleton moved, it had an odd, lop-sided gait, as if one of its legs was shorter than the other. The candlelight wobbled as the skeleton struggled awkwardly down the steps.

And then the boys heard a voice that was like nothing they had ever heard before. It was kind of scratchy, like a gate that hasn't been oiled, and gritty, like a rock being dragged along a cement sidewalk. And old-sounding, like Oren's great-grandfather just before he died.

"My foot," the skeleton moaned in that horrible voice, but softly, as if it were coaxing something

47

from a bit of cottonwood fluff. "Give me back my foot."

Jimmy Joe grabbed hold of Oren, and Oren hung on to Jimmy Joe. Both of them were so frightened they couldn't move. The skeleton was slowly coming closer, and it was like its empty eye sockets could see them.

The boys scrambled to their feet and began running as fast as their own running shoes would carry them. You might have thought they would have raced home. But to do that, they would have had to run past the skeleton.

Instead, they ran in the other direction.

No matter how fast they ran, whenever they glanced back they could see the skeleton, still holding a flickering candle, hard on their heels. In fact, it was getting closer and closer.

"FOOT," the skeleton moaned in a voice that was louder and even more horrible sounding. "GIVE ME BACK MY FOOT!"

Soon they were smack dab in the middle of

that big swamp that circled around the town. They splashed through some slough water and scrambled up a bank that was all tangled with cypress and willow roots.

Jimmy Joe looked back. The candlelight in the skeleton's bony hand was so close now that it seemed to blind him.

"GIVE ME BACK MY FOOT!" the skeleton called out in a voice so loud and awful that it sent owls flapping from their perches and coyotes yipping into the night.

"I haven't got your foot!" Jimmy Joe hollered.

"THEN I'LL TAKE YOURS!" the skeleton roared, and Jimmy Joe felt a bony hand grab his ankle. He went sprawling headfirst into a hollow and he felt a terrible pain as that skeleton twisted away at his foot. Jimmy Joe cried out, and the candlelight seemed to go dancing away in that couple of seconds before everything went black for him.

"Heavens to Betsy," Carolina Giddle said, yawning and stretching her arms. "It's about time you two were in bed."

"You can't quit there!" the boys called out. "Tell us what happened. Did the skeleton get Jimmy Joe's foot?"

Even Barkus, curled at Carolina Giddle's feet, gave a sympathetic "wuff," as if he, too, wanted to hear what happened next.

"All right." Carolina Giddle sighed. "Once you've brushed your teeth and have your pajamas on."

In three and a half minutes both boys were back on the sofa, flashing their scrubbed teeth, tugging their pajama tops and bottoms into place.

You remember that old lady? The one who lived just back of the Chattahoochee? Well, when Jimmy Joe screamed and fell, Oren raced on as fast as he could go. It was that old lady's house he came to first.

When the breathless boy managed to get enough of his story out, she grabbed her shawl and a lantern, and the two of them headed back.

Oren fully expected to find Jimmy Joe lying there minus a foot. But when they found him, it looked like a root tangle had wrapped itself around one of his ankles. That's what had caused him to trip.

The old lady carefully unwrapped the root as Jimmy Joe regained consciousness, crying out, "My foot! I want my foot!"

"You've got both your feet," the old woman said. "But this one is badly sprained. You both should know better than to be running through the swamp at night."

"But the skeleton — " Jimmy Joe sputtered.

"Look!" Oren pointed to a light flickering through branches some distance away.

The old woman clucked her tongue.

"Swamp gas," she said. "You can see that most nights. Here, lean on me. We'll get you back to my place and put a splint on that ankle."

The odd thing was, that same night the hundred-year-old foot disappeared from the medical lab where it was being studied. And no one ever saw it again. When Jimmy Joe's foot was strong enough to walk on, he went with his daddy to work, and he checked the closet where he had found the skeleton.

And do you know what he found?

Nothing.

I guess that skeleton, once it had both of its feet, decided it was time to take up residence somewhere else. Some place where no one would be making off with any of its bones.

As Carolina Giddle finished her story, Mr. and Mrs. Fergus could be heard at the apartment door.

"Everything okay?" Mr. Fergus looked

suspiciously at the boys in their pajamas on the couch.

"Hunky dory," Carolina Giddle said. She placed Chiquita's cage carefully in her bag beside the empty bone-rattler container.

"Candles?" Mrs. Fergus eyed the sputtering tea lights on the end table.

Dwight stretched and yawned. "The lights went out in the living room," he said.

"A fuse," Dwayne added.

As the two headed down the hall to their bedroom, Dwight lifted his hand in a backward wave.

"G'night." Dwayne picked at a piece of bone rattler stuck to his pajama top and popped it into his mouth. "Swamp gas," he mumbled, the words slipping past the peppermint taste on his tongue.

"Swamp gas?" Mr. Fergus scratched his head. Mrs. Fergus stared after the retreating boys as if she had never quite seen them before.

Later, Carolina Giddle slipped into the sunroom that rested like a glassy cage against the edge of the Blatchford Arms. There was only a sliver of a moon, so very little light shone in. She turned on just one of the table lamps. She liked the near-darkness. The room was a comfortable spot for sipping a cup of something hot before going to bed.

Tenants over the years had donated odd bits of furniture. Carolina Giddle's favorite was a wing-backed chair the color of hominy. And there was an old phonograph in one corner that she had grown fond of. It had a handle to crank and played the old black records she remembered from when she was a little girl visiting her grandmother. There was a stack of these.

She put one on now. It was scratchy, but the melody came through faintly like the fuzzy moonlight seeping into the room.

In my sweet little Alice blue gown...

"One of my favorites," whispered a voice.

"Mine, too," Carolina Giddle whispered back.

THREE
Shadow Killer

IT WAS A MID-AFTERNOON in late November when Carolina Giddle rang the doorbell at the Croop apartment.

"Oh, my!" Mrs. Croop said, eyeing the babysitter's coat and hat and gloves. "Did you just come from out-of-doors?"

"No." Carolina Giddle smiled a big smile. "But it's such a lovely day I thought the children might like to go out for a while. I've never known it to be so warm with December just a week away."

"Yes...yes..." Mrs. Croop was a nervous little woman who only came as high as

Carolina Giddle's chin. She had a habit of re-peating herself and fluttering her hands as if she was juggling the extra words. "Outside for a walk. Not too late, is it? The dark, you know. Hubert and Hetty — well, especially Hubert — doesn't like..." She lowered her voice to a whisper. "The dark. Spooks him, the dark! I was like that, too, when I was his age." She giggled and then clapped a hand over her mouth.

"Say hello to Ms. Giddle, children."

"Hello, Ms. Giddle." The children glanced up at the babysitter and then shyly returned their gaze to the checker board.

In a flurry, Mrs. Croop grabbed her wrap from a chair. "I'm late for meeting Papa. Be good for Ms. Giddle." She fluttered her fin-gers in a good-bye wave. To Carolina, she said, again in a whisper, "Sylvester and I have a meeting of the Save the Pigeons Society — and we serve the refreshments and do the clean-up after. We shouldn't be too late but, if we're not back, see that the children are in bed by nine. Remember to leave the lights on in their rooms, though…you know…it's what they're used to." She eased the door shut as she left the apartment.

"Is it an exciting game?" Carolina Giddle inquired.

"No," said Hetty. "But our TV is out for fixing."

"Won't be back 'til Tuesday," Hubert added glumly.

"I have an idea." Carolina Giddle pulled her sweater coat closer around her. It was orange and warm looking, the color of a ripe pumpkin. "Why don't we go for an outing in the park? It's still early, and such a lovely afternoon, considering it's November."

"I dunno." Hubert looked suspiciously at the living-room window. "It'll be getting dark soon."

"Land's sake!" Carolina Giddle laughed. "There's least a couple of hours of good sunlight. We can have a picnic." She patted her large bag. "I've got cocoa in a thermos. And Rumpelstiltskin sandwiches."

"Rumpelstiltskin sandwiches?"

"My daddy used to make these when I was little. We didn't know what to call them so I named them." Carolina Giddle smacked her lips. "They're made with banana bread and marshmallows and chopped-up mini chocolate bars. You know, the kind that people give out as Halloween treats? I always have a bunch left over."

"Mommy left us a snack," Hetty sighed. "Carrot sticks and parsnip hummus."

Hubert gave a little groan. "Okay," he said. "Let's go."

Carolina Giddle was right. It was still sunny as they entered the park. They walked along the trail that followed the shoreline of a small lake in the middle.

When she noticed Hubert looking apprehensively at the patches of darkness in the shaded treed areas, Carolina Giddle began to sing.

"There's nothing better than campfire songs when you're out for a brisk walk. *'A horse and a flea and three blind mice...'*"

So they sang. It took seven songs to get them to the best picnic table. It sat in the sunlight, well away from the shade of evergreens.

By the time they were ready to head home, the sun had begun to go down. It was beginning to get a bit chilly, too. Hetty put on her mitts and hung onto Carolina Giddle's gloved hand — the one that was not occupied with her going-to-the-park bag. Hubert kept so close to Carolina Giddle's sweater coat, he might as well have been wearing it himself.

A long shadow from one of the park's statues stretched across their path. The statue was of a famous musician holding his violin, but to Hubert the shadow looked like a zombie with an ax sticking out of its head. He cringed and closed his eyes as they walked over it.

A little farther on, they came upon another shadow. This one, cast by one of the pylons by the park gate, was gigantic. Hubert, with his eyes closed, strayed from the path, stumbled over a water fountain pedestal and fell into the middle of the dark mass.

At that moment, a jogger ran by. He was accompanied by a dog the size of a bear. Drool dripped from its muzzle. Hubert let out a howl that brought an answering howl from the dog.

"Land sakes alive!" Carolina Giddle said, handing her bag to Hetty. She helped Hubert to his feet. His teeth wouldn't stop chattering. He held her hand all the way back to the Blatchford Arms.

"Papa always reads to us before we go to bed," Hetty said, after dinner and baths.

She began hunting through the bookshelf. "There's *Perky the Pigeon* and *A Pigeon Keeper's Guide to Carrier Training.*"

"Well, now," Carolina Giddle declared, "I'm a better teller than I am a reader. You just find yourselves the most comfortable spot on that sofa and tuck that afghan blanket around you. I'll make us all some honey hickory tea."

Once the children were tucked up with the afghan, Carolina Giddle went around the apartment, turning off lights.

"What are you doing?" Hubert whimpered.

"Too much light is bad for storytelling." Carolina clicked off everything in the living room except for a small table lamp by the sofa. Then she reached into her going-to-the-park bag and pulled out a plastic container of round candles in tiny tin pans.

"Candlelight is the best."

She arranged the candles in a large flat

ornamental dish Mrs. Croop kept on the coffee table.

In a minute, candles were lit and she was back with mugs of steaming hickory tea for all of them.

"Now, let's see…" Carolina Giddle took a sip of her tea. Flames from the candles flickered and danced. "A story for a November evening…hmmm. I think you might like hearing about the mountain king and the shadow killer."

Hubert shivered and pulled the blanket tighter as Carolina Giddle began.

This is the story of a boy I knew a few years back. Jack Scrumble lived with his grandfather up on the side of Cornshuck Mountain. How old are you, Hubert? Seven and a half? And you're a year older, Hetty? Well, Jack had just turned nine.

He was pretty brave for a nine-year-old. He helped his grandfather rescue sheep that sometimes stumbled down a steep incline at the edge of their pasture. Looking down from that ledge could make you dizzy as a hornet that's fallen into a mint julep. When his granddad gathered honey from their hives, Jack was right there giving him a hand, never mind he'd been stung twice by honeybees. He learned to milk their cow, Adeline. She was a miserable beast who was known to kick out at you if you didn't approach her in just the right way. A bruised shin didn't keep him from doing the milking chore.

But one thing Jack didn't like was the dark shadows that ranged over Cornshuck Mountain. Once the sun began to sink, it seemed that wherever Jack went he was met by horrible shadows from twisted pine trees and odd-shaped rock outcroppings. The shadows looked as if they might be made by trolls or werewolves, or maybe even dragons.

What Jack didn't know was that Cornshuck Mountain was ruled by a mountain king who, *as mountain kings go, wasn't all that bad. Except for one habit. He liked to spend time dreaming up scary shadows when he should have been tending to a hundred and one other things that needed doing.*

Like what?

Well, a good mountain king makes sure all the mountain streams and waterfalls are working — not plugged up with rocks and dirt and leaves. He's responsible for painting mountain ash berries that color of orange-red that looks like the heart of a candle flame. He polishes up quartz crystals so they can wink at the moon on a dark night.

Like I said, a multitude of chores.

To tell the truth, the mountain king's wife was getting fed up with tending to most of these chores herself. Meanwhile, her husband played around, twisting tree branches so they made shadows that looked like hairy mammoths or zombies with three heads.

"Zeb," she announced one evening, after she had spent the entire day teaching a litter of young mountain wolves how to yodel, "time you quit all that shadow work. I know you come from a long line of fright-masters given to spooking travelers who should know better than to be out on mountain paths at night. But that band of crooks is gone and there are no more moonshiners making bootleg liquor. So there's really no reason —"

"There's that boy," the mountain king said. "You should have seen the expression on his face when he was hurrying home from the sheep corral and I cast that shadow that looked like a Tyrannosaurus rex. Oh, my, I thought I'd die laughing!"

Yes, the mountain king's wife thought. You're spending all that time scaring one little boy when you could be lending him a hand. Coyotes needed to be shooed away from the sheep. Their old milk cow could use some guidance finding a good patch of clover.

"What if that boy can't be frightened any-more?" she said. "Will you give up all of this shadow-play nonsense?"

The mountain king smiled to himself. He knew that he could come up with shapes that would have Jack Scrumble quaking in his boots for years to come.

"Certainly, dear," he said. "If you can get him to walk a mile along the Cornshuck Trail at sundown. You know that stretch from the sheep pen to his cabin. Get him to walk that without his teeth chattering or without breaking into a run as if a banshee is after him. Then I'll give up shadow-making."

"Agreed," said his wife.

The next day, while the mountain king was spending his time contorting tree branches to look like giant snakes and arranging rocks into hunchbacked horrors, his wife made a visit to the Scrumble farmhouse. She disguised herself as a traveling saleslady selling soaps and cosmetics.

"Don't have much need for none of them trap-pings," Granddad Scrumble told her when she came to the door. *"We make our own soap and we still have half a bottle of Grandma's rose at-tar perfume. Ain't been opened since she passed over. But come on inside. We don't get many visitors up on Cornshuck these days. Jack here'll put the kettle on and make us all a cup of tea."*

The mountain king's wife liked to spend time with company herself, so she enjoyed her cup of tea. Granddad told her about the special recipe he had for making soap with beeswax and juni-per berries.

"And what do you like to do, Jack?" she asked.

Jack ducked his head and scuffed his shoe on the pine floor.

"Whittlin'," he admitted.

"He's mighty good at it, too. Can make a wil-low whistle that'd charm a mockingbird down from its nest." Granddad paused and lit his pipe.

"Jack," he said, *"time to go and check on the*

sheep. The days are gettin' shorter, remember. You don't like to be out when it's gettin' dark."

Jack's complexion went as white as the doily that sat under the teapot on the table.

"Yes, Granddad." He hurried and got his jacket.

"I'll be on my way, too," the mountain king's wife said. She walked Jack out to where the path to the sheep pen forked away from the main road.

"Oh, my. I almost forgot." She stopped and unlatched her sample case. "I always leave a little gift whenever I visit prospective customers. So this is for you." She took out something shiny that looked like a pen, and as she gave it to Jack, she whispered something in his ear.

Jack smiled. "Gee, thanks," he said and tucked the pen in his pocket.

By the time Jack got to the sheep corral, the mountain king's wife had joined her husband. He was waiting just back of a pile of boulders that bordered the path. The sun was low in the sky, and the mountain king had arranged the rocks in such a way that they looked like a shadow cast by a huge wolf.

In a few minutes, Jack would be heading the mile back home along this path. The mountain king chuckled at how menacing the shadow looked.

Jack shooed a stray sheep back into the corral. He fed the two orphan lambs and then counted the rest of the flock to make sure none were missing.

Latching the gate, he tested it with a shake to make certain it was secure. He had heard wolves yipping and yodeling earlier in the day. He wanted to be extra sure there was no way they might get into the pen.

As he turned and started back along the path, he noticed the sun was only a skim of molten gold along the mountain peak. The trail ahead was strewn with shadows.

Jack gulped. An owl hooted. A few feet down

the path a huge dark shape loomed across the
trail.

It looked like a giant wolf.

In the distance an animal howled.

Aaarrooooo...

Jack closed his eyes. How was he ever going to
make it home?

OOoooh-Aarooooo... The animal howled
again.

Was it close enough to create that shadow just
up ahead?

Then Jack remembered the pen.

He pulled it out and flicked a small switch on
the cap. A beam of light streamed out. As Jack
approached the wolf shadow, he shone the beam
onto it. The shadow skittered and scattered. The
wolf's gaping mouth disappeared when Jack
played the light against it. Its ears flew away,
and Jack could see the clay of the trail, looking
the way it always looked. The wolf's tail, dis-
solved by light, turned into clumps of crabgrass.

In a minute, Jack was past the shadow.

He heard another sound. But it didn't sound like a wolf howling.

In fact, it was a groan from the mountain king, but Jack didn't know that.

Farther along the trail, more shadows crossed the path. One had wavy tentacles like those of a giant octopus ready to coil around its victim. A huge spider settled in the midst of a crookedy web. Farther on there was a horrible witch-head with a long nose and a pointed chin.

But Jack's shadow killer — a pen light — slew all of these monsters. He laughed and whistled as he walked that mile back home.

The mountain king and his wife went home, too — to their cave high up on the mountain. As the king settled into his easy chair with his pipe and the latest copy of the Cornshuck Chronicle, *his wife cooked their supper of bacon, grits and mountain greens.*

"I guess I'll spend tomorrow making sure all the echo points are still working well along the east canyon," the king sighed.

"And then you can give that grove of pines on the south slope a good shaking, so they drop their pine cones. It's that time of year." The mountain king's wife stirred her hominy grits and sighed with satisfaction.

Hubert sighed, too. He was actually leaning against Carolina Giddle. If only, he was thinking…

Carolina Giddle stirred and stretched and gave a little pull on one of her crystal earrings. The tea candles were sputtering. A couple had already gone out.

"Can you guess what I have in my bag?" she said.

Hubert and Hetty looked at her, wide-eyed.

"Not… " Hubert stammered.

"Yes, indeed." Carolina Giddle got her

bag from the hallway and came back with two pens in her hand. "The mountain king's wife visited me, too. I bought a whole batch of these from her. So here's one for each of you. Now let's see if they work."

She tilted the shade on the table lamp, so that when she placed her hands in front of the bulb, it made a large shadow on the living-room wall. In a minute, she had arranged her fingers in such a way that the shadow actually looked like a wolf's head.

Hubert and Hetty didn't have to be told to flick the switches to turn on their pen lights. They played their lights against the shadow.

"Yes!" Hubert exclaimed, waving his hand so that the light skittered all over the walls and ceiling.

He thought he heard a wolf whimper.

But maybe it was just the radiator making one of its funny noises.

Carolina Giddle gave the old heat register a little tap.

In the hall there was a sound of metal groaning and moaning.

"I think I hear the elevator," she said. "Bet it's your mom and dad. Best get my things together."

———

That night, Carolina Giddle didn't go down into the sunroom with her cup of rosehip and raspberry tea. Instead she went to the parking lot. Trinket was in a stall near the gate where a street lamp shone down on her. Bits of glass — necklace beads, crystal charms, strapless watch-faces — glinted and winked from the lovely clutter of the Volkswagen's coat.

"Howdy, old gal." Carolina Giddle gave her an affectionate pat. "I had a lightning bolt thought today. You and I are going on a little jaunt. Over to the Blatchford seniors' home. Don't know why I didn't think of it before."

It was after midnight when the car chugged into the circular drive in front of the residence. The building was dark, but the old-fashioned post lights by the front entrance cast a soft light over the nearby benches tucked into shrubbery.

Carolina Giddle was not particularly surprised to see a woman as old as you can imagine and as wispy as the evening mist sitting on a bench.

"Aunt Beulah." Carolina Giddle greeted the old woman warmly as she got out of the car.

"Carolina." Aunt Beulah's voice was soft and crickety as a hickory branch scratching against a windowpane. "I been waiting for you."

"I should have known."

"I'm not very mobile," Aunt Beulah apologized. "Gertie took away my wheelchair soon as I passed over."

"You just take my arm," Carolina Giddle said, "and we'll get you into the car."

FOUR

Eyes of the Movie Monster

"WHERE ARE YOU going, Daddy?" Elsa Lubinitsky was practicing the Volga Boat Song on the piano. She stopped to watch her father arrange his jacket collar so that it was even all around. He ran a comb through his tangled curls.

"Insane." He turned and winked at her. "I'm going insane."

"No. Really."

"On a date." He changed his mind and flipped the jacket collar up. "Dinner. A concert." He made a face at himself in the mirror. "A date with Miss Peebles. You know — the lady who works at the art supplies store."

"Oh." Elsa played another line of the Volga Boat Song. Miss Peebles had a voice that sounded like she'd just sucked in air from a helium balloon.

"Can we go?" Luba, Elsa's younger sister, whined. With one hand she waved a sheet of paper with an outfit she'd designed for a giraffe cut out of a *National Geographic* magazine. In the other, she poised some scissors so the blades made a V.

"Me, too." Five-year-old Galina jumped up. She'd been drawing a scaly bat-winged monster on a sheet of paper her father had given her from his portfolio case.

"You munchkins!" Rubin Lubinitsky laughed. "I told you. This is a date. Your poor father needs to get out once in a while."

"So that's why you smell like vanilla ice cream." Elsa rolled her eyes. "Ooh-la-la!"

"Ooh-la-la yourself, you goof. It's aftershave. You're supposed to smell like vanilla ice cream when you go on a date."

"Gots on your shiny shoes," Galina observed. She couldn't resist trying her felt marker on one of the toes to see if it left a mark.

"How come your pants are all sharp down the middles?" Luba put down her giraffe and ran a finger along the creases.

"They're going-out-to-dinner pants. So you look good sideways." Their father heaved a sigh. "Now, no more questions. Better yet, let me ask a question. Has anyone seen my keys?"

"Not me." Galina grinned. But she couldn't help glancing at the sculpture they all called the Wonky Dish Man. It did have something like an empty dish for a head. It collected many things. Balls of plasticine, Cheerio bracelets, loose change. And keys.

"There." Rubin plucked his car keys from the Wonky Dish Man's cranium. "Your father is ready to roll."

"Who's going to stay with us?" There was a tremor in Luba's voice. She hoped it wasn't Mrs. Byle, who smelled like an ashtray and always made them go to bed by seven-thirty.

"Ms. Giddle." Rubin leveled a look at his three daughters. "And no tricks. You're not to use my acrylic paints to decorate the fridge door or any other appliances. And no carving anything out of soap. No sharks or candle-holders. Knives are verboten. Elsa and Luba, I expect you to keep an eye on Galina. You know how she can — "

The doorbell rang.

"There's Ms. Giddle now," Rubin said, folding his collar down. As he went to open the door, he grabbed a fedora from the hall stand to cover some of his wild hair.

Carolina Giddle wore a shawl that made Elsa think of a spiderweb that had got out of control. In fact, it was pinned at her shoulder with a brooch shaped like a spider.

"Hey!" Luba shouted. "You're the lady with the funny car!"

"Don't be rude. And be careful with those scissors." Rubin gave Luba a stern look. To Carolina Giddle, he said, "If the girls are exceptionally good they can stay up a bit late tonight. Since there's no school tomorrow."

"Yay!" Elsa banged the lid down on the piano keyboard.

"Bye, Dad!" they chorused as he slipped out the door.

Carolina Giddle patted the bag she'd brought with her. "I wasn't sure what we'd want to do this evening so I brought some games and playing cards. Let's see, there's Snakes and Ladders and — "

"Let's play Mix 'n' Match!" In her excitement, Luba came pretty close to jabbing Carolina Giddle with the scissors still attached to her hand.

"Mix 'n' Match? Don't tell me you have a

game I've never heard of." Carolina shook her head in amazement, and a strand of her flyaway hair escaped from a dragon-shaped clip and popped onto her forehead. "I thought I knew all the games in the world." She eased the scissors away from Luba's fingers.

"It's easy," Elsa began. "You take some blank sheets of paper…"

"Let me tell." Luba tugged at her sister's sweater. "You gotta fold the paper into threes and… "

So that's what they did. Mix 'n' Match.

There was no shortage of drawing paper in the Lubinitsky apartment. After all, Rubin Lubinitsky made his living as an artist. Carolina Giddle folded each piece into even thirds as the girls explained that each player — in a secret corner — would create a funny character. The character's head would be in the top third of the paper; the body in the middle; and the legs and feet in the bottom. Once they were finished, they would cut along the folds and then mix and match the body parts to make even crazier characters.

When it came time to cut and reassemble the pieces, Galina held onto the monster she had drawn on her paper.

"No!" Galina screamed when Luba tried to take it from her. "Don't cut him up!"

So, while Galina stayed in her corner and hummed a little song to her monster, the others took turns taping body parts together to make weird and wonderful creatures.

"This is the most fun I've had since we played double-dare dressup with my cousins when I was about your age, Luba." Carolina Giddle was holding her sides with laughter as Elsa added huge, clumpy hairy feet to a lady wearing an elegant cocktail dress. The lady's head looked like it might belong to a witch. But the witch had flyaway hair and dangling crystal balls hanging from her ears.

"Uh-oh," Luba shrieked. She pointed at the corner where Galina was humming. With magic markers, she was drawing a monster on a canvas. Rubin Lubinitsky had primed it with white gesso earlier in the day, getting ready to begin a painting.

Galina's new monster had fiery hair that looked like bedsprings, pointy ears and a mouth with vampire teeth. It had scales on its arms and legs, and claws instead of fingers and toes. Bat wings sprouted from its shoulders.

She was just about to draw in the eyes when Carolina Giddle said gently, "You may not want to draw in the eyes, Galina."

"Why?" Galina held on stubbornly to her marker.

"Well, I'll tell you. But first we need to clean up our Mix 'n' Match mess. And, Galina, I see a can of white gesso there that you could use to cover up your monster. I'm sure your sisters would help you."

"No!" Galina glared at them all.

"Don't look at me." Luba scowled back at her sister.

"We're trying to teach her consequences," Elsa explained. "She makes a mess, she cleans it up."

"All I can say…" Carolina Giddle looked seriously at the three of them. "Is that we're luckier than a handful of four-leaf clovers that Galina never drew in those eyes."

"Why?" Galina reluctantly lay down her marker.

"Teeth brushed and into your nightclothes first."

"Can I wear my Wild Things pajamas?"

"Of course, sweet pea."

It took the better part of an hour to clean everything up, to get into pajamas and to have their bedtime snack. Carolina Giddle had brought squiggies — crunchy squares with jelly fillings all the colors of the rainbow that gave off little explosions of chocolate as you ate them.

"Now, you can each have one more squiggy if you promise to nibble very quietly. And I'll tell you the story about the eyes of the movie monster."

The girls snuggled up on the sofa.

Carolina Giddle fetched a mesh cage out of her bag.

"This is Chiquita," she said, "my pet tarantula. She's fond of a good monster story." Chiquita nodded her hairy head and did a little run around her cage that made the girls squeal.

But Carolina Giddle hushed them quickly. "Don't encourage her or she'll be showing off all evening."

Chiquita settled down, snacking on a couple of dead flies and a tiny piece of squiggy square that Galina was allowed to slip into her cage. Carolina Giddle licked a bit of melted chocolate and jelly off her own fingers before she began.

This story was told to me by an old man. Diego del Monterrey worked in the special effects department of a movie studio where I worked many years back.

"*Do you remember those monster movies from the early days of sound pictures?*" *he asked me one evening when we were all working late. We were waiting for the moon to come out from behind some clouds for a night shoot.*

"*Oh, yes,*" *I said.* "*I was too young to see them at the theaters, of course, but I loved watching them on TV when they came on the late show.* Dracula *and* Frankenstein *and* The Wolf Man."

"*Well,*" *Diego said,* "*you never saw the scariest one of all.* The Scaly Batmonster of Scuggins Creek."

He was a young man back then, hardly more

than a teenager, working at one of the Poverty Row studios. They made really cheap movies, and the head of the studio, Clifford B. Mizer, was the cheapest and nastiest studio chief you might ever run across. When he saw how monster pictures were raking in tons of money at a studio across the way, he thought it was something he should try.

"Get that young artist Diego del Monterrey working on it," everyone told him. "He's amazing." Diego's grandfather was Mexican. He had shown him how to capture creatures of the imagination on paper. One of his best was a dragon-man with a long spiky spine and tail, who could breathe fire out of his nose. And then there was Electroman, who shot electricity out of his fingertips and glowed in the dark.

"But be careful with the eyes," his grandfather always said. "Unless you say a blessing as you paint in the eyes, the creature may rouse itself to life and become a true monster."

So, whenever Diego came up with a new creature, he said his grandfather's Mexican blessing as he drew in the eyes.

When Clifford B. Mizer saw Diego's paintings, he became very excited.

"Yes! Yes!" He had a high squeaky voice like a mouse. "These are marvelous! But I want something huge, gigantic. Bigger than Frankenstein, scarier than Dracula."

Diego pulled one more painting out of his portfolio.

"How about this one?"

It was the most horrible monster you could imagine. Squiggly hair coiled from its head like wire springs sticking out of an old chair. It had pointy ears and wings like a giant bat. Its arms and legs were scaly like a snake's skin, and it had sharp claws like an eagle.

"Marvelous!" Clifford B. Mizer squealed. "I want you should paint it on something as big as the wall in Soundstage Ten. We will bring in

people and see how frightened it makes them."

"I will need money," Diego said. He was making next to nothing as a boy who helped move cameras and sound equipment around. Barely enough to pay his rent, much less buy groceries. Dinner was often nothing more than a radish sandwich and a cup of tea.

"Yes, yes," the studio boss squeaked impatiently. "You will be paid. Now you should start. Don't waste a minute."

Diego hunted up a huge piece of canvas and stretched it on a wall in Soundstage Ten. He had to use a ladder to sketch in the upper part of the monster. It took him several days. People from the studio would come by at lunch or after work just to see how it was coming along.

"Ooh, those vampire teeth, how horrible!" they would say with a shiver. "And those bat wings! I can almost hear them flapping!"

When Clifford B. Mizer's niece came to look at the painting as Diego was adding the finishing

touches, she screamed and hid her face in her uncle's coat.

"How can anything have such awful scaly skin and claws!" she sobbed.

"Wunnerful! Wunnerful!" said the studio boss. "I want it should give you nightmares. The more horrible your dreams, the more money I make."

Diego was glad to hear him mention money. The next day was payday. He was anxious to see what Clifford B. Mizer would give him for this creation that was going to make him millions.

He was on his ladder, painting in the creature's greenish face, when the studio boss and his accountant came in the next day.

"That's very good," Mizer said. "I've arranged a fifty-dollar bonus for you."

Diego felt sick to his stomach. "Fifty dollars? But I thought —"

"It's really just a painting." The accountant stepped forward and smiled up at him. "We *have to do all the work now, creating the Bat-monster."*

For a month Diego had been dreaming of how the Scaly Batmonster was going to be his ticket to a better life. Fifty dollars! It was nothing. They might as well have knocked the ladder over and given him a few good kicks.

"I quit," Diego hollered down at them. "But, wait. First I'll just finish up the monster's face. I've yet to paint in the eyes."

As he silently began painting in the left eye, he noticed that the canvas began to shiver a bit on the wall. It was as if some unseen force was moving it. There was a muffled sound, too. It was like the caw of a huge crow trying to work its way through a sore throat.

Crrawww.

Diego heard Clifford B. Mizer gasp.

He carefully worked in the monster's other eye.

As he completed the last brush stroke, the creature began to stir from the canvas. Diego could feel the scales as its belly expanded into life. His ladder toppled, and he fell smack atop the startled accountant, who cried out and then began to whimper.

Clifford B. Mizer stood beside them like a statue. And they all watched in horror as the monster struggled free of the canvas.

Crraww.** There was nothing muffled about its roar now. It was as loud as a locomotive going through a railway tunnel. **Crraaaww.

"No eyes on my batmonster," Galina said, looking over at the creature she'd drawn on her father's canvas. She curled against Carolina Giddle and stuck her thumb in her mouth.

"Consequences," Luba repeated, looking sternly at her sister. "Galina should get to work and fix — "

"Oh, be quiet. I want to hear what happened next," Elsa muttered. "Did the batmonster eat everyone up?"

Carolina Giddle smoothed the curls on Galina's forehead.

"Not exactly…"

There was a scrabble of the monster's claws as it began tearing around the soundstage, knocking over props and movie equipment. It was like a giant vulture trapped inside a cage. A smell issued from it that can only be described as a hundred rotten eggs exploding. They could hear the flapping of its huge bat wings as it tried to find a way out.

Electrical cords snapped. Sparks caught on the mess of spilled paint, turpentine and shredded canvas. One whole side of the soundstage exploded into fire. Clifford B. Mizer began to holler for help as he grasped the trunk of a fake tree.

Diego was able to free himself from the accountant's clutches. He raced to the soundstage entrance, where he worked the levers that opened its huge doors. He leaped back just in time to escape being caught by the Scaly Batmonster's claws as it stampeded through the opening.

Diego watched as it spread its wings and took off, gradually disappearing into the clouds. Clifford B. Mizer and his accountant hurried out after him.

By this time Soundstage Ten was fully aflame. They could hear the sirens of fire trucks rushing to the studio, but it was a windy day. In no time at all the flames spread to the other buildings on the lot.

When Clifford B. Mizer told everyone what had happened, they said he was crazy. The police and the insurance company insisted he'd lit the fire himself. The accountant disappeared (some say with a suitcase full of the studio's money), and no one ever saw him again.

"And I never said a word," Diego told me. "Clifford B. Mizer got just what he deserved."

Luba sighed and stretched. "Did anyone ever see the batmonster again?"

"Only one or two people who happened to make the mistake of drawing the creature in places where they shouldn't."

Galina pulled her thumb from her mouth, slipped down from the sofa and marched over to the canvas. The large tin of white gesso was still out on the plastic work-mat beside the easel, but she couldn't figure out how to pry off the lid.

"Here, I'll help you," said Luba.

Elsa rummaged through her father's supplies and found a couple of paintbrushes.

"Me, too," she said, handing one of the brushes to Galina.

It took about half a can of gesso, but the monster disappeared.

Carolina Giddle found her two friends in the sunroom that night. She told them about her evening and nibbled on the last piece of squiggy square as she sipped her tea. The two shook their heads and laughed softly.

"Brings to mind some of my own antics." The young woman smoothed the lace on her white dress. "I remember Willard Strutt and I playing Truth or Dare. He took my dare and fell off the porch roof at school. I had such a crush on him. All those blond curls and freckles. Cute as a bug's ear. I think you got to know him, Beulah."

"Oh, yes. He was one of the boys at Ada's Halloween party. The night...well, you remember. The night you...intervened."

"Intervened?" Carolina Giddle gave her crystal earrings a slight shake.

The old woman and the young woman exchanged glances.

"It's quite a tale." Grace brushed her hand

over Carolina Giddle's. It was like the touch of a gentle breeze. "Bears telling…but some evening when you're not tuckered out from babysitting."

"Yes," Carolina Giddle said. "You know how I love a good story."

FIVE
Ghost Ship

"*O mio babbino caro*," Mama Bellini trilled as she swirled into the living room in her red going-to-the-opera dress.

"Bellissima!" Papa exclaimed, slicking back his hair and straightening his bowtie. "Look, children. Look at how beautiful your mama is. She should be on the stage tonight!"

"Oh, Papa!" Mama Bellini gave him a kiss on the forehead.

"I wanna go, too," Angelo Bellini scowled.

"Sweet baby." Mama Bellini hurried over to hug her five-year-old. "When you're bigger you can go. Right now opera is just for Mama and Papa, yes?"

Angelo pushed his mother's hug away and opened his mouth.

For a second everything was quiet in the Bellini apartment. Angelo's older sisters, Amanita and Corrina, looked at one another and gritted their teeth. Mama's hand swooped to her forehead as if she were trying to ward off a headache. Papa closed his eyes and shook his head.

It only took a second. Then Angelo uttered a scream that shook the ceiling lamp and sent the Bellini dog, Alfredo, whimpering for cover under the couch.

"I wanna go!" Angelo howled. He screamed again, so loud that no one heard the doorbell.

It was only when he stopped to draw breath that they heard someone knocking.

Mama and Papa both grabbed their coats as they headed to the door to admit Carolina Giddle.

"Ohgoodyou'rehere." Mama's words were moving even faster than her high-heeled opera shoes. She nearly knocked Carolina Giddle over at the doorway.

"We'll be back before midnight." Papa gave Carolina Giddle a nervous smile as he eased past her.

By this time Angelo was not only screaming nonstop but was stamping his feet faster than a dog trying to get at a flea with its hind leg. The radiator began clanging in time to his dance. Neighbors on both sides of the Bellini apartment were pounding on the walls.

Carolina Giddle hurried in, picked up the little boy and held him so close that his hollers were muffled in her frizzy sweater.

"Hushabye, hushabye," she crooned, but Angelo managed to give her a couple of kicks. "Mercy me!" Carolina Giddle exclaimed as she released him. Angelo crumpled onto the rug, sobbing and banging his head against the floor.

"He's always like this," Amanita sighed. She was four years older than Angelo. "Maybe we can put him up for adoption."

"Or take him camping and forget to bring him home," said Corrina, who was a year and a half younger than Amanita. "Time out doesn't work. He throws fits that are the worstest in the world."

"Well," Carolina Giddle drawled, "he may think he throws the worst fits of anyone who has ever lived, but Angelo isn't a patch on the Tantrumolos."

"The Tantrumolos?" Amanita and Corrina said.

"Yes, the Tantrumolos. I'll tell you about them, but first..." Carolina Giddle reached into her bag. She pulled out tea candles, a can labeled *Ghost Host: The Drink That Soothes,* and a plastic container filled with dessert squares. "I just this afternoon baked up a batch of granghoula bars. My mother showed me

how to make them when I was just your age
and we lived on a little island off the coast."

Angelo had quit banging his head and was
crouched on the floor crying softly enough
that he could hear what Carolina Giddle was
saying. He even paused totally as the babysitter displayed one of the bars and mentioned
the ingredients. Strawberry jam and crushed
chocolate cookies, pecan nuts and green
maraschino cherries with a ghostly cap of
whipped white icing.

"An old sea captain who lived on the island
told me about the Tantrumolos," Carolina
Giddle continued as she put the kettle on and
arranged the tea candles on the coffee table.
"If I'm going to tell you the story the captain told me about the Tantrumolos and the
ghost ship of the Southern Seas, it's best told
by candlelight."

Carolina Giddle looked over to where
Angelo crouched, scowling.

"If you're going to continue with your fit, Angelo, please keep to the other side of the room. We need to be safe where candles are involved. If you get tired of the fit, there's a place beside me on the sofa. And, girls, once you have your drinks and granghoula bars, find a spot and get comfortable. While you're getting settled, I'll just bring Chiquita up for a bit of fresh air."

She reached into her bag and produced a cage that contained a tarantula spider. Chiquita scampered over to the mesh wall for a closer look at things.

It only took Angelo a minute to scoot across the room and confront the arachnid nose to nose.

"This is one of Chiquita's favorite stories," Carolina Giddle said. "She won't want to miss it."

When Barney Boonswagger was a young man sailing the South Seas — he wasn't a sea captain yet, of course, just a deckhand — the old sailors liked to tell tales of a mysterious sail-ship they saw at times. There have been stories of ghost ships for as long as men first began coursing the seas in boats of one sort or another. But Barney took little stock in these tales spun over cups of rum in the twilight.

One night he was taking his turn on watch, up on the deck of a small cargo vessel, when the fog crept in. It was the kind of fog some sailors called a pea-souper — so dense that you could barely see a hand in front of your face. Someone at the ship's helm sounded a foghorn, and every few minutes, that mournful **whooo** *rolled out into the night.*

That's when Barney thought he heard someone crying somewhere out on the water.

"Help me!" the voice came, so muffled by the fog that it sounded like someone trying to holler with a woolen scarf over his mouth.

"Help me!" The voice was louder and closer.

Clinging to the railing, Barney peered over as far as he could, to see if he could make out who was crying for help.

And that's when the strangest thing happened.

It was a calm sea, with the ship moving slowly and steadily through the shroud of fog. But all of a sudden the vessel lurched, as if it had been suddenly pushed by a giant hand, and Barney fell over into the sea.

He called out as he fell, but at that moment the foghorn sounded and drowned out his cry. Then, for what seemed like an eternity, he was plunging downward through the water. In desperation, he began to struggle to the surface. With his lungs almost bursting, he crested and drew breath. He was hoping to see the side of the cargo ship close by, hoping that he could hear its engines.

But there was nothing. All he could see was the fog swirling around him. Everything was eerily silent.

He hollered for help. His call sounded exactly like the one that drew him to the ship's railing and then into his plunge overboard.

The fog began to clear a bit, and Barney gasped to see that he was only a couple of feet away from the wooden hull of a ship. A rope ladder was being lowered over its side. Swimming the few strokes to where the ladder dangled just above the water, Barney grasped the first of the rope rungs and gradually worked his way up.

What do you think he saw as he flung himself over the railing and onto the deck?

"What?" Angelo said. He had inched his way along the floor and now sat right beside Carolina Giddle's feet.

He reached for a granghoula bar and began licking the icing off its top.

Well, it looked like a whole crew of ghosts, but not a crew such as Barney had ever seen. These looked like they might belong in a pirate movie, except they had an ashy white appearance. As they moved about the deck, some of them seemed to disappear into wisps of fog and then reappear a minute later as the fog shifted.

All of them were scowling.

"Who…who are you?" Barney stuttered.

One of the crew, who had the largest three-cornered hat perched over a scarred brow, growled, "We are the Tantrumolos of the dreaded ship Horribilis.*"*

"And you are our entertainment," said another ghostly figure. This one wore an eyepatch and packed a huge pistol in one hand. "I decide how you will die this evening and join our crew."

Before Barney could say anything, a sailor with a wooden leg and a hook in place of his left hand yelled, "I'm the one who saw him at the railing, just ripe for the picking. I say we make him walk the plank. We haven't had a good plank-walking for a hundred years."

At this, the ghostly sailor with the hat began to jump up and down.

"I'm the captain," he hollered. "And I want him keel-hauled. Run him underneath the ship a couple of times."

"No, it's my turn," the ghost with the eyepatch screamed. "You killed the last one. Remember? Flogged him to death." He pointed at a sad-looking shadowy figure at the ship's helm.

"MINE!" the captain screamed and drew his sword. He lopped off the good hand of the Tantrumolo with the hook. The ghostly hand flew through the air and began slapping the captain across the face.

The wounded Tantrumolo howled, "TAKE THAT, YOU POCK-FACED BILGE RAT!"

The ghost with the eyepatch raised his pistol and yelled, "MINE! MINE! MINE! I'M THE ONE WHAT KNOCKED THE SHIP AND GOT HIM INTO THE BRINE!"

He shot holes into the others, which didn't

seem to have much effect, being as they were already ghosts. But it did make them even madder.

In no time the entire crew of the Horribilis had become a whirlwind of ghostly sailors screaming at one another. Swords clanged. Oaths flew along with knives and buckshot.

"DIE, SCUM! MEET YOUR MAKER, YOU MURKY MUSKETEER!"

"I'LL SWASH YOUR BUCKLE, YOU BILIOUS BABOON!"

Barrels of rum were thrown about and smashed so that Barney had trouble staying upright on the slippery deck. Ripped sails fluttered down like ribbons. Even the ship itself seemed to heave and groan.

Barney decided that anything was better than staying aboard the Horribilis, and he leaped over the side.

Bits of flotsam and jetsam were scattered around where he landed in the water. He grabbed hold of an empty barrel that kept him afloat.

115

Gradually the ghost ship and its horrible screams and yelling and musket fire drifted away, and Barney was all alone, floating in that silent sea.

That's when he saw a most welcome sight — a light growing brighter by the minute. Yes, it was a rescue boat that had been sent out from his ship when the crew realized a man had fallen overboard.

"Here!" Barney called out. "Over here!"

Of course his rescuers were anxious to know all that had happened to him in the couple of hours he had been missing.

"If I told you," Barney said, "you'd never believe it."

"And so he didn't tell anyone until many years later, long after he'd quit sailing the seven seas. He told me when I was just about your age, Amanita." Carolina Giddle brushed a lock of curly hair back from Angelo's forehead as he leaned against her arm and nibbled a last little bit of granghoula bar.

"Bilge rat!" Angelo giggled.

"Yes." Carolina Giddle gave him a little tickle. "And now it's time for everyone to be off to bed."

"Aagh." Corrina clenched her teeth and gave a little moan.

"You said the b-word," Amanita whispered. She put her hands over her ears.

But Angelo just yawned, waved goodnight to Chiquita and said, "You gonna tuck me in, Carolina Giddle?"

The apartment was as quiet as a tomb except for some contented little clinks from the radiator when the Bellinis returned.

"I can't believe it," Papa Bellini said in a hushed voice.

"You're a magician," Mama Bellini added.

"No. Just a storyteller," Carolina Giddle replied as Mr. Bellini pulled out his wallet to pay her.

––––––––

Carolina Giddle's work for the evening wasn't quite finished. A little later she rang old Mrs. Floss's doorbell.

"We have three people for the séance," Mrs. Floss said excitedly as she ushered Carolina Giddle into her apartment. "Mrs. Chan is hoping to get in touch with her grandmother, and Mr. Winkle is just here for support." She lowered her voice to a whisper. "And for some of my dandelion wine."

The four joined hands at the card table Mrs. Floss had set up. Carolina Giddle closed her eyes. For a few minutes everything was silent except for the sounds of the old people breathing. Then Carolina Giddle nodded her head at Mrs. Floss.

"Your husband says to tell you he misses you and he hopes you found someone to go square dancing with."

"Oh, my." In the dim candlelight, it was possible to see a twinkle in the old lady's eyes. "We did love to go dancing."

Mrs. Chan's grandmother only spoke very little English, so it was more difficult to pass on a message from her.

But what surprised Carolina Giddle was a voice she hadn't called up.

"That little house from long ago," the voice crooned. "Where blackbirds sing and daisies grow,/Beyond the bend on the old bayou/Someone's a waitin' there for you."

Carolina Giddle had known only one person in her life who spoke in rhymes, and he had died thirty years ago. He was a dockworker with eyes the color of nutmeg. She remembered the rough feel of his hand when he held hers.

Now she blushed as she sipped a glass of Mrs. Floss's dandelion wine.

SIX

Alien Ghosts

"ON THE TOP floor. It's the closest we could get to outer space," Benjamin Hooper breathlessly informed Carolina Giddle when she asked him where he lived. He and his sisters were coming out of the laundry room as Carolina Giddle was going in.

"I've seen spaceships from my bedroom window. Always late at night, round about two in the morning. You know how people say they're like saucers? They aren't. They're more like flying hotdogs but with rows of lights where the wiener goes. Hotdogs flying sideways. The power source is probably right in the middle which makes sense because it would be protected by the top and the bottom, and the extraterrestrials' quarters would be there in the middle too in case there was any, like, you know, flying space debris that might…"

Benjamin had finally run out of breath. His older sister, Lucy, set down the laundry basket she was carrying. She sighed and shook her head.

"Benjamin is space crazy," she said. "He can talk for hours about outer space…"

"And exterterriswheels," Emma, Benjamin's younger sister, added.

"That's me!" Benjamin grinned and zoomed a detergent container back and forth in his hands as if it were a planetary rover from a space shuttle. "Aliens are my primary interest. I don't think I'll be a regular astronaut when I grow up but more of a researcher-detective tracking extraterrestrial incursions…"

"You must tell me more when I come up to babysit on Sunday evening." Carolina Giddle flashed a smile at the three children.

"Will you tell us a story?" Lucy asked. "We heard you always tell ghost stories."

"If you're sure you won't be frightened."

"Yay!" Emma did a pirouette and dropped her armload of towels.

"Phooey." Benjamin brought the soap bottle to a sudden halt. "I'd sooner hear a story about aliens."

Carolina Giddle hefted her laundry hamper to her other side. "We'll have to see what settles into the storytelling air of the evening. My grandma always said you can feel a good story coming the same way you can feel a good ice cream coming when you first hear the tinkle of a Dickie Dee bell."

On Sunday evening, even as his parents were leaving phone numbers and instructions with Carolina Giddle before they headed out the door, Benjamin was packing his collection of model spaceships into the living room. He wanted Carolina Giddle to have a full viewing of his collection.

"Don't touch them, Emma," he warned. "You know what happened to my Mars climate orbiter."

"But I needed a treadmill for my Barbies."

"Perhaps you can help me clear a space to put out some snacks, Emma." Carolina Giddle opened her large handbag. She drew out a lumpy plastic grocery bag and a couple of plastic containers.

"And, Lucy, could you find me a plate for these Martian Munchies?" Carolina Giddle held up something round and green, like a tennis ball flecked with icing sprinkles. "I hope none of you are allergic to popcorn."

"Not me! I'm not bellergic." Emma did one of her little twirling dances perilously close to another of Benjamin's models. "What's in these?" She stopped and tapped her fingers over Carolina Giddle's containers.

"Well, let's see. In this one I have delicious frozen alien worms."

"Eww, worms." Lucy made a face.

"From Venus." Carolina Giddle toyed for a minute with her silver hair clip. It looked like a giant dragonfly. "Worms are a great delicacy to the Venusians."

"Well, actually…" Benjamin gave a little yank on Carolina Giddle's sweater. "It's very unlikely that there are worms on Venus. The Russians thought they spotted a scorpion but scientists have decided it was just a lens cap that fell off some of their equipment."

"There is much yet to be explored on Venus," Carolina Giddle said knowingly.

Emma opened the lid on the other container.

"Oh, wow," she giggled. "These look like bugs, too."

"Jupiterian Jumbles," Carolina Giddle said. "Very healthy. I make them with carrots and celery and peanut butter."

It took Benjamin the better part of an hour to present all of his space models to Carolina Giddle. Lucy and Emma busied themselves with a game of Chinese checkers, careful to lick peanut butter and green icing off their fingers as they moved marbles over the playing board.

"Hey!" Benjamin finally noticed the snacks were disappearing. "Save some of those for me."

"Yes, it is your turn to take a little sustenance," Carolina Giddle said. "Why don't we all find a comfortable spot around the coffee table? I'll light a few candles, and we'll need to find a spot for Chiquita."

All the children in the Blatchford Arms had heard about Chiquita.

"She's fond of a good ghost story," Carolina Giddle noted.

"Is it your birthday?" Emma asked, eyeing the candles as she crunched the head of a Jupiterian Jumble.

"Oh, dear, no! But candles always help me to focus when I'm telling a story. I call it the incandescence factor."

When they were all settled, and Chiquita was chewing on something that looked suspiciously like a real worm, Carolina Giddle began.

"This is a story my Aunt Bedelia told to me when I went to stay with her for a couple of months when I was ten — about your age, Lucy. She lived in Roswell, New Mexico — "

"Roswell!" Benjamin jumped up from his cushion and nearly stepped on his model of the Starship *Enterprise*. "That's where some UFOs crashed and they found bodies of aliens but the army said they weren't really extraterrestrials — "

"Yes, Benjamin, you're right. But you must be as quiet as a stealth plane, or this story will never get off the ground."

Aunt Bedelia did live right where those sightings were said to occur. There is a good deal of debate about what actually happened, but no matter what anyone reports, Bedelia — who was about twelve years old in 1947 — never forgot what she saw and heard one night…

They lived on the edge of town, and their yard backed right out onto the desert. That night Bedelia's dog ran out of the yard. Bedelia saw Muffin racing away, dodging cacti and jimson weed. Bedelia went after him, even though she'd been warned by her parents not to go out into the countryside by herself, especially at night.

The last glitter of sunset sat on the horizon like a thin ribbon of dying radiance, and already Bedelia could see a full moon rising in the desert sky.

"Muffin!" she called. "Muffin!"

She heard him bark in the distance, but she couldn't see where he was.

Bedelia figured she must have walked for about half an hour when she finally stumbled into a small gully. Muffin was there at the bottom, crouched, whining at something half hidden by a stand of creosote bushes.

There was a whitish glow to whatever it was that was hiding. Eerie, like captured moonlight.

Oddly, Bedelia wasn't frightened. But a strange feeling came over her. Something like sadness.

"Here, Muffin," she called softly, and the dog turned and looked at her as if he, too, were pained by what he saw.

Slowly, Bedelia made her way down to him and gave him a reassuring pat.

"Who's there?" she said, her voice quaking just a little bit.

As the evening darkened, the glow intensified slightly, and Bedelia became aware of a strange sound.

Who...owooo. *It was kind of a cross between an owl's hoot and a baby crying.*

Who...owooo.

Muffin's whine blended in, making the sound even more melancholy.

"I won't hurt you," Bedelia said.

Slowly, a creature emerged from behind the creosote bushes. It was no bigger than Bedelia herself, and humanoid in shape. It had a very large head. The glow it emitted seemed to pulse like a light from a generator when it is running low on power.

In one hand, it held a tubelike object.

"Who...what are you?" Bedelia asked.

The creature tilted its head a bit and gave her a puzzled look. At least it had stopped its mournful crying. It reached up and rubbed a finger against a panel on its chest. A small rectangle

on the panel pulsed on and off. Then the creature spoke in a voice that sounded like it was being created by a machine.

"I am Maroo," it said.

"Where do you come from?" Bedelia asked.

"From home," the creature said in a strange artificial voice followed by a small sob that definitely didn't sound like a machine. "I am lost."

"Lost?"

"Our ship was intercepted and we crashed. I was on it with my father."

Bedelia was so sorry for the creature that she reached out to give him a comforting pat. Before she could touch him, though, the tips of her fingers tingled as if they were zapped with a cold current. She drew her hand back quickly.

"You can come home with me and we can send for help," she said.

"I want to find my father." Maroo's head swiveled to the left and then to the right. Bedelia *noticed moisture seeping from one of his large almond-shaped eyes. "Will you help me look?"*

"I'd like to help you but I don't know where to begin."

"Would your companion know?" Maroo looked at Muffin, who was lying down on a patch of sandy soil by the creosote bush.

"Muffin?" Bedelia gave a small laugh. "Muffin's just a dog."

"I can ask him?"

"I'm afraid dogs don't speak."

But then Muffin surprised her by rising and wagging his tail and barking.

Bedelia watched as Maroo's finger scanned the panel on his chest and found another small rectangle that pulsed.

"Rroof, roofff, ruff ruff," Maroo barked.

"Rrooff woof," Muffin barked back. He headed away from them slowly, toward the west.

"He knows where to go," Maroo said to Bedelia.

"*Maybe he does.*"

Bedelia and Maroo followed Muffin.

They had been walking for about a quarter of a mile when they noticed flashing lights. Something was happening up ahead.

They came to the crest of another gully. When she looked down, Bedelia could see some army jeeps from the base nearby and a couple of ambulances.

The vehicles were at the edge of a wreck of some sort. There was a mass of twisted metal. It was strange metal like a cross between aluminum and fish skin. The lights from the army vehicles gave the wreck a silvery glow. Bedelia noticed what appeared to be rows of small windows in a part of the craft that hadn't been so badly damaged — windows that scattered the light back at the soldiers and the medics milling around.

She heard a gasping sound from Maroo. Medics were carrying something out on a stretcher.

It was a creature that looked exactly like Maroo.

Its eyes were closed. Black liquid seeped from a wound in the side of its head. She saw Maroo's hand go up to the side of his own face as if he expected to find the same liquid oozing there.

Somehow Bedelia knew that the slight figure on the stretcher, so completely motionless, was dead. Muffin whimpered.

Then they noticed another stretcher being carried out of the wreckage. On it was a figure similar in shape and appearance to Maroo but quite a bit larger. There was a gash across this creature's chest and more of the black liquid. But the creature's eyes were open. One of its hands moved to touch the wound.

Maroo uttered a strange cry, like something caught in a machine.

Although it was hard to tell from that distance, Bedelia was certain the creature looked up to where they stood at the crest of the gully. Then its eyes closed, and its arm and hand fell limply to the side of the stretcher.

At the same instant, it seemed to Bedelia that something soft and glowing rose from the stretcher. The misty glow moved toward them. As it ascended the walls of the gully and moved farther and farther away from the activity around the wreck, it took on definition. It became a duplicate of Maroo only larger. Glowing as Maroo did. White, luminescent.

Maroo ran down to meet the figure. They clasped each other in a ghostly hug. By Bedelia's side, Muffin wagged his tail and sighed softly. They watched as the two figures moved away from the crash site, as if they were being drawn by some unseen force. In minutes they were no more than two flickering lights in the distance, like a couple of fireflies in the night.

Oddly, without Maroo at her side, Bedelia felt suddenly frightened. She turned and hurried for home with Muffin scurrying along behind her.

"Where have you been?" her mother said

crossly when she got home. "I've told you not to be running around outside after dark."

"Muffin got lost," Bedelia said, "but I found him."

Something kept her from telling her parents what really happened that night.

She knew they would just think she was making up stories. And in the morning, she half wondered if it was something she'd dreamed.

When she and Muffin trekked out to the site the next day, there was no trace of the crash. The sand was oddly smooth and devoid of plants, as if it had all been carefully swept.

As they headed back, Muffin stopped at the crest of the gully where Maroo had stood with them and watched his father pass away on the stretcher below.

Muffin whimpered. He nudged Bedelia toward a jimson weed with something caught in its underbranches. It was the small tubelike object Maroo had been carrying. In the daylight, Be-

*delia could see exactly what it was — a model
of a spaceship.*

"Does your aunt still have the model?"
Benjamin asked, his eyes transfixed.

"No, she doesn't." Carolina Giddle shook
her head. The dragonfly clip in her hair
winked at them in the flickering light from the
tea candles.

Benjamin sighed. "I bet it was something.
Too bad she lost it."

"She didn't," Carolina Giddle said. "She
gave it to me." Reaching into her handbag,
she pulled out a box.

Emma and Lucy leaned forward.

Benjamin reached out, his fingers shaking
as they brushed the lid of the box.

"Go ahead," Carolina Giddle said. "Open
it."

Inside, nestled in tissue paper, was the
model.

It looked a little like a hot dog, with a double row of tiny windows where the wiener would go.

———

Later, Carolina Giddle ran into Herman Spiegelman as she was getting out of the elevator on the main floor.

He clicked off the vacuum cleaner. "You like to come down here to the sunroom at the end of a day, don't you? If you got any tea left over you can always tip it into the aspidistra pot. That plant thrives on tea."

It wasn't until the caretaker had finished and headed to his suite that her friends appeared.

"Have you heard any more?" Grace was barely visible this evening. "You know, from the rhyming man?"

"Not heard, but I have a feeling I should —"

"Your mama always said no one had itchier feet than you." Aunt Beulah shook her head. "Me, I was never one to travel much farther than a frog can spit."

Carolina Giddle sighed. "If I'd known he stayed right there all these years..." With a finger she stroked the crystal in her left earring. "But let's not talk about that. Tell me, Grace, about that Halloween just after you died."

"Oh, yes, that Halloween. But you should tell it, Beulah."

"I'll never forget it." The old woman took a deep breath. "That night of Ada's party..."

SEVEN

The Elevator Ghost

IT WAS HALLOWEEN night, and Carolina Giddle was giving a party.

"She's having it in the sunroom," Corrina Bellini said to Hetty Croop as they compared their invitations.

Each invitation was shaped like an eye-mask. Corrina's had a tiny black cat on each corner and was dusted with gold sparkles. Hetty's had a small jack-o'-lantern between the eyes.

"She told me her apartment was too small for everyone," said Hetty, who was dressed as a ballerina. Red sequins spotted the nylon net of her tutu like a glittery rash of measles.

"Are you guys going to tell a ghost story?" Benjamin Hooper asked. All of the mask-shaped cards invited the guest to tell a ghost story — if they wanted to. "I'm calling mine 'The Ghost Spaceship.'" Ben was dressed as a UFO. He looked out at the girls through his space goggles.

"I'm telling a story about a vampire dog that loves to drink cat blood," Corrina said.

"I just want to listen," Hetty said shyly.

The three joined a parade of children streaming through the sunroom door. Awful-looking spiderwebs drooped from its upper corners. Hubert Croop shuddered and smoothed the cardboard feathers of his owl costume.

The room was decorated with items the children had helped make the day before. Dwayne Fergus's jack-o'-lantern, with its Dracula teeth and slitty eyes, grinned from the snack table.

Dwight had constructed a swamp monster out of milk jugs and ice-cream containers taped together with duct tape and painted green. It was covered with drips of snotty slime he'd made by mixing mint toothpaste with engine oil. Eerie lights gleamed through its eyes and mouth.

One of Galina Lubinitsky's drawings of a scaly bat monster was tacked on the wall above the aspidistra. The monster wore a mask over its eyes.

"She puts masks on all her monsters now," Luba explained.

Luba and Elsa had made funny Mix 'n' Match creatures. One had a head like a fairy-tale princess, a middle like an overweight heavy-metal rock star, and legs like Sasquatch.

The older Lubinitsky sisters wore costumes their dad had helped them create. Elsa was a Picasso painting with two huge eyes on one side of her face and a round striped tummy. Luba wore a costume covered with pictures of clock faces that looked like they were melting.

Galina, to no one's surprise, was dressed like a bat monster. Scales had been carefully sewn on her pajamas. Her bat wings, made out of black garbage bags attached to wire coat hangers, drooped a bit in the back.

Lucy Hooper put on a record of "Danse Macabre." Emma Hooper and Angelo Bellini twirled and danced beneath a disco ball that caught the light from tea candles artfully arranged between a large wing-backed chair and a stool against the far wall.

The snack table was covered with Carolina Giddle's specialties. There was a tray of Rumpelstiltskin sandwiches and plates of purple squiggy squares and iced granghoula bars. Peppermint bone rattlers filled a ceramic bowl covered with small ghosts. Another

huge bowl, as black as a witch's cat, was filled
with green popcorn balls.

"Martian Munchies," Emma Hooper whispered to Amanita Bellini.

Frozen alien worms lolled in ice cubes
floating in a punch bowl of lemonade. An urn
was filled with Carolina Giddle's hot Ghost
Host brew.

But where was Carolina Giddle?

Herman Spiegelman, wearing his usual
work clothes, was keeping an eye on everything. He made sure no one stood too close
to the candles or got into a food fight at the
snack table.

"He doesn't need a costume." Dwight
nudged his twin.

"He looks like that guy who gets the bodies
for Frankenstein," Dwayne agreed.

Suddenly all the lights in the sunroom went
out. Gasps and small shrieks circled the floor
like surround sound.

When the lights came on again several seconds later, Carolina Giddle was sitting in the wing-backed chair.

Another gasp, like the breath of a ghost, rippled through the room.

Carolina Giddle's hair was white with a couple of white cloth roses tucked into the curls. Her face was the color of chalk, and her eyes were rimmed with black. Blackish-red lipstick outlined her mouth. She wore a long lace-trimmed whitish dress of some thin material that looked like it could have been spun by spiders. It was torn and tattered in places.

She made a beckoning gesture with her hands, and everyone in the room drew closer.

"Y'all make yourselves comfortable," Carolina Giddle said in a voice that sounded a little crackly, as if she had put it on to go with her ghost dress. There were chairs and floor cushions close to where she sat.

"Now, is everyone ready for our ghost-story extravaganza?"

There was a chorus of yesses along with some moans and little shrieks.

"Me first!" Angelo Bellini shouted. No one argued. He'd been better since Carolina Giddle had been babysitting the Bellini children, but he could still throw a pretty amazing tantrum.

"This isn't a whole story," Angelo said as he climbed onto the storytelling stool. "It's a…what?"

"A riddle," Amanita Bellini prompted.

"Yeah. A widdle." Angelo inhaled a big breath of air. "Where do baby ghosts go in the daytime?" Before anyone could hazard a guess, he hollered out, "A dayscare center!" and quickly climbed down off the stool, a big smile on his face as everyone laughed.

Benjamin was next.

"There was this spaceship," he began, "and

it was sort of like the Orion Multi-Purpose Crew Vehicle except it had eight tail blades, not four, and the front cone had a sensor spike sticking out of it sort of like a narwhal horn…"

It took him fifteen minutes to tell the story.

"Wake me when it's over," Dwayne said halfway through.

Then Lucy Hooper took over the chair and told a story about a spooky hitchhiker who had four thumbs. Hers only took five minutes.

There were six stories in all, followed by a break for snacks. The ice cubes in the punch bowl had melted and a fat worm candy hung out of Angelo Bellini's mouth. The room was filled with the sound of crunching bone rattlers and granghoula bars. Dwight and Dwayne Fergus's tongues turned green as they licked the sparkles off their popcorn balls.

Herman Spiegelman dimmed the lights. The tea candles next to Carolina Giddle flickered excitedly.

It was time for Carolina Giddle to tell her ghost story.

When she was a young girl, my great-aunt Beulah lived here — in Apartment 712 — right across from where I live now. The Blatchford Arms, in those days, was the fanciest apartment building in the city. People would sometimes come just to ride the elevator which, you have to admit, still looks pretty fancy even if it does creak and moan like a banshee on a bad night. Imagine how shiny it all was a hundred years ago when everything was new — the marble tile on the floor, the brass bar for hanging onto, glass frosted with designs that looked like the feathers of exotic birds.

Beulah had only been living in the building for a couple of months when she met Ada, who lived

149

on the fourth floor. They became best friends. When Halloween rolled around that year, Ada's parents let her host a masquerade party.

The girls spent weeks getting ready for it.

Beulah devoted a lot of time to her costume. She was dressing up as Pierrette, a kind of clown figure you might see on the stage back then. She talked her mother into buying her some white silk pajamas, and she attached black pompoms to the buttons of the pajama jacket. With pipe-cleaner wire and starched handkerchiefs, she created a ruffle for the neck, and on her head she wore a black skullcap from Chinatown. She painted her face white with clown makeup and applied perfect pink circles to her cheeks. She darkened her eyebrows and outlined her eyes with black eyeliner. She was something to see!

It took quite a while to get ready, and Beulah knew guests would already be arriving down in Ada's apartment. So she hurried into the hallway to catch the elevator. The arrow above the elevator *gate indicated it had to come up from the lobby.*

As she waited, Beulah looked out the hall window onto the lawns and gardens below. This was back in the days before a parking lot circled the building.

It was a perfect Halloween night. A full moon bathed the scene below her with a silvery glow. At the edge of the garden, children had built a bonfire. She could hear their faint laughs and shouts as they tossed dead branches and bits of broken furniture into it.

But then she became aware of another sound. A closer sound.

Someone coughing. It seemed to be coming from behind the door of Apartment 713.

That was very odd, because that apartment belonged to the Van Rickenhoffs, the family that owned the building, and they were never there. It had been closed up, Ada told Beulah, ever since the Van Rickenhoff daughter, Grace, had died from consumption the year before.

Could the family have returned without any-one realizing it?

Cough. Cough.

Maybe it was just the radiator in the hall.

Cough. Cough.

No, it was definitely coming from someone just behind the door of Apartment 713.

Beulah looked at the arrow above the eleva-tor gate again. It had moved up to the number 4 on the dial. Likely people getting off for Ada's party.

Cough. Aargh. Cough.

The hacking cough made Beulah twirl around, and she was amazed to see the door to 713 slowly open.

A young girl stood in the doorway. It looked like she was dressed as a ghost for Halloween. Her face was almost as white as Beulah's clown-face makeup. There was a feverish glow to her blue eyes, made all the brighter in contrast to the gray hollows beneath them. A couple of silk flowers were woven into her pale hair. She was wearing a white dress trimmed with lace.

"I'm wondering if you could help me?" she said to Beulah in a voice that was hardly more than a whisper.

"Of course," Beulah said. "Are you going to Ada's party?"

"A Halloween party?" the girl said. Then she smiled. "I love your costume." She brushed her fingertips over the neck ruffle. "Can you help me fasten this corsage to my shoulder? The pin keeps slipping for me."

She handed a cluster of white silk flowers to Beulah. It looked like some of the petals were beginning to come loose. Beulah tried to tuck them back in and bind everything together with a faded pink ribbon that dangled from the corsage.

When she took the pin, she was startled by how cold the girl's fingers were. And when she pinned the corsage to the dress, she felt the same icy cold on the girl's shoulder.

"There," Beulah said. *"If you're going to Ada's, we can go down together. What's your name?"*

The girl smiled. "The elevator is almost here," she said. She closed the door to the apartment behind her and stood beside Beulah.

The elevator stopped, making a funny wobbly noise like it always did, as if it couldn't decide exactly how to match its compartment floor with that of the apartment hallway.

It finally eased to a full stop.

"At last!" Beulah laughed nervously. She unlatched the wrought-iron gate.

And that's when something very strange and unexpected happened.

The girl gave Beulah a violent push that sent her sprawling to the floor. Then she hurried into the elevator and pulled the gate closed.

"Hey, what are you doing?" Beulah hollered. She could see the girl through the glass.

Before the elevator started to move, it looked

155

like the girl opened her mouth in a kind of a cry. You know how it is when you've really hurt yourself and you're starting to cry but no sound comes out for a couple of seconds? That's what the girl looked like.

The elevator began to move.

Suddenly there was a horrible wrenching noise, and the sound of metal grinding. Beulah realized the elevator was plunging downward with nothing holding it back.

It only took a few seconds before there was a crash that reverberated throughout the building.

Beulah raced down the stairs. Doors were opening in the hallways, and people hurried along with her. At the fourth floor, Ada, dressed as a Spanish dancer, was in the midst of costumed people from the party.

She grabbed Beulah by the sleeve. "What happened?"

"The elevator fell!" Beulah began to cry, tears streaking through her white makeup. "And

there was a girl in it. I…I was almost in it my-self but she pushed me back!"

It only took a couple of minutes for them to make their way down to the basement. Sure enough, there was the wreckage of the compartment in a tangle of twisted cable and bent brass, with splinters of wood and shattered glass thrown about.

Beulah turned away. She felt she wouldn't be able to stand seeing what had happened to the girl in the white dress. There was no possible way anyone could have lived through such a ghastly accident.

But then she heard one of the men in the crowd say, "Lucky there was no one in it."

Could she have heard him correctly?

Beulah went over to the wreckage. The man was right. It did not contain the broken body of the girl. All she found as she bent closer to the floor was one small white silk rose.

"My great-aunt Beulah picked it up and kept it in a box with her jewelry all her life, and when she passed away, she left everything in that box to me."

Carolina Giddle reached up and plucked a white rose from her hair.

"I have it to this day," she sighed. "Aunt Beulah always said there must be such a thing as good ghosts, although that was the only ghost she ever met. She and her friend Ada were certain that somehow Grace Van Rickenhoff, who had died from consumption — TB as we know it — sensed that the elevator was about to make its last trip. She was determined that Beulah would not be in it when that happened."

"They cough," Herman Spiegelman said to himself. "Consumptives. A rattling cough, like an old radiator."

"Apartment 713," Lucy Hooper whispered to Hetty Croop. "That's where Carolina Giddle lives. Right across — "

Carolina Giddle rose from the wing-backed chair and stretched. She touched the pale silk roses of her corsage and smoothed the lace that trimmed the neck of the old white gown she wore.

"I will be mighty disappointed," she said, "if there is a single bite left for me to carry up from the snack table. Take those leftovers up to your parents. I have my bag here and the bowls and trays fit quite nicely into it. We must thank Mr. Spiegelman for cleaning up once we are gone. And for being the light-master for our ghost-story gala."

"Goodnight!" everyone cried out as they wrapped the remaining goodies in paper napkins to take home. "Happy Halloween!"

Only Dwight and Dwayne Fergus still planned to go out trick-or-treating at this late hour. They grabbed their pillowcases, stashed behind the aspidistra.

Carolina Giddle was no longer in her costume when she came back down to the sunroom an hour and a half later. It had been cleared of its Halloween decorations and the furniture put back in place.

"You didn't tell the whole story," said an old crackly voice from the shadows. "You didn't tell how, over the years, Grace and I became friends."

"My stories are often a bit raveled," Carolina Giddle said. "I just tuck the loose threads back in best I can to make a tidy edge."

She wandered over to the old gramophone.

"Put on 'After the Ball,'" Grace said softly. "I was pretty shook up from that elevator plunge, but of course you can't really hurt a ghost. So I slipped into Ada's party later that night. Everyone was dancing to 'After the Ball.' It was so lovely."

Carolina Giddle found the record and put it on.

"We're going to miss you," Aunt Beulah said, her words caught up in the old waltz.

"I'll miss you, too," Carolina Giddle said.

It was close to midnight when Dwight and Dwayne got back to the Blatchford Arms.

A crescent moon looked like it was leaning against the east tower of the old apartment building.

"Hardly worth going out," Dwayne complained. He pulled off his Freddy mask. At most houses porch lights were off and no one was answering to a cry of "Halloween apples!"

"Do you think there's still some of Carolina Giddle's treats left?" Dwight yanked down his Scream mask. "We could load up and — "

The boys paused, speechless. In the No Parking space in front of the Blatchford Arms lobby door sat a trinket-scabbed Volkswagen wearing a huge cap of odd stuff. They could make out the arms of a coat rack, an upside-down armchair, a mattress, cardboard boxes, and some rolled-up rugs. It looked like a yard sale all tied together with bright scarves and braided rags and ropes.

And there was Carolina Giddle handing something to Herman Spiegelman just before she climbed behind the wheel of the bug.

"Hey!" Dwight shouted. But the Volkswagen was already easing its way out of the lot.

The twins watched as it paused at the main road and then turned south.

When they got to the lobby, Herman Spiegelman was still there. He was looking out to where Carolina Giddle's car had been a few minutes earlier, as if he was waiting for her to change her mind and come back.

"Where did Carolina Giddle go?" Dwight asked angrily, as if it was all the caretaker's fault.

"I'm not sure." Herman Spiegelman sighed. "She said she was heading back to where she'd once lived. She said it wasn't so much reason as rhyme that was calling her. No idea what she meant by that. But she left this for us to take care of. We can keep her in her cage here in the sunroom by the aspidistra."

Herman Spiegelman pulled off a bright calico bandana covering Chiquita's home. The tarantula looked at them. It seemed she waved one of her hairy arms agreeably before crawling under an aspidistra leaf the caretaker had plucked and tucked into the cage.

The caretaker shook his head in a way that grown-ups sometimes do when the ways of the world seem well beyond them.

"She said Chiquita had grown really attached to the Blatchford Arms and didn't want to leave."

"I don't care if she doesn't come back." Dwight mumbled.

"But she will," said Dwayne. "She'll miss Chiquita."

He placed the bandana gently over the cage.

"Won't she?"

Afterword

Probably for as long as people have told tales, scary stories have been popular. In front of a cheery campfire or on a comfortable sofa, it can be fun to listen to the hair-raising adventures of others.

Carolina Giddle comes from a part of North America where ghost stories have thrived — the Southern United States. She builds some of her own tales on the framework of stories she might have heard herself as a child. But she borrows from other sources, too. We know she loved old horror movies such as *Frankenstein,* but echoes of newer

movies also creep into her babysitting sagas
— Johnny Depp's Caribbean pirate pictures;
films about extraterrestrials such as *E.T.* and
Close Encounters of the Third Kind. I won-
der how she came across the Chinese legend
about a painting of a dragon that springs to
life when the artist paints in its eyes?

Roswell, New Mexico, offers its own in-
triguing accounts of a possible UFO crash and
cover-up. There could well have been ghosts.

As for Carolina Giddle's trinket-covered
Volkswagen, I suspect she must have visited British Columbia at some point and
been enchanted with poet Susan Musgrave's
decorated vehicle.